PENGUIN BOOKS

PROPHECY OF THE UNDERWORLD

Low Ying Ping is the author of the *Mount Emily* novels, a middle-grade/ young-adult fantasy series featuring time travel and friendship. The first book, *Mount Emily*, was shortlisted for the Hedwig Anuar Children's Book Award 2018 and the second book, *Mount Emily Revisited*, won the Singapore Book Awards 2017 in the Middle Grade/Young Adult category. Three of the books have also been shortlisted for Singapore's Popular Readers' Choice Awards. *Mount Emily* was also selected for inclusion in the National Arts Council of Singapore's Read Our World: SingLit Book Gift for Schools.

She has also written an English adaptation of the Chinese classic *Journey to the West*, for children aged seven to ten years old. Her short story, 'The Age When Magic Begins', won second prize in the British Fantasy Society's short-story competition 2018. Her poems and critical essay have appeared in *Singa*, the journal of the National University of Singapore Centre for the Arts, and *QLRS* (*Quarterly Literary Review Singapore*). She holds a Master's degree in English Literature from the University of Warwick, UK.

Prophecy of the Underworld

Low Ying Ping

PENGUIN BOOKS
An imprint of Penguin Random House

PENGUIN BOOKS

USA | Canada | UK | Ireland | Australia
New Zealand | India | South Africa | China | Southeast Asia

Penguin Books is part of the Penguin Random House group of companies
whose addresses can be found at global.penguinrandomhouse.com

Published by Penguin Random House SEA Pte Ltd
9, Changi South Street 3, Level 08-01,
Singapore 486361

First published in Penguin Books by Penguin Random House SEA 2022
Copyright © Low Ying Ping 2022

All rights reserved

10 9 8 7 6 5 4 3 2 1

This is a work of fiction. Names, characters, places and incidents
are either the product of the author's imagination or are used fictitiously,
and any resemblance to any actual person, living or dead, events or
locales is entirely coincidental.

ISBN 9789814954167

Typeset in Garamond by MAP Systems, Bangalore, India

www.penguin.sg

Table of Contents

Part - I   1

   Chapter One   3

   Chapter Two   11

   Chapter Three   22

   Chapter Four   32

   Chapter Five   40

   Chapter Six   49

   Chapter Seven   60

   Chapter Eight   68

   Chapter Nine   75

Part - II   83

   Chapter Ten   85

   Chapter Eleven   92

   Chapter Twelve   98

   Chapter Thirteen   102

Chapter Fourteen   110

Chapter Fifteen   116

Chapter Sixteen   123

Chapter Seventeen   130

Chapter Eighteen   143

Part - III   155

Chapter Nineteen   157

Chapter Twenty   168

Chapter Twenty-One   175

Chapter Twenty-Two   181

Chapter Twenty-Three   192

Chapter Twenty-Four   201

Chapter Twenty-Five   210

Acknowledgements   215

For my brother.
Thank you for the laughter.

Part - I

CHAPTER ONE

I had always known that if one day the world needed saving, Matthew Pane would be the one to do it.

Matthew was this incredible boy-wonder we had in our school. At thirteen, he was already a star badminton player, had won first place in the National Junior Chess Competition, knew all the answers to the questions the teachers asked in class and even to those they didn't, was warm and firm and kind all at the same time, and inspired love and respect and loyalty from everyone who knew him. He was the sort of person who, if confronted with the choice to save either the world or his best friend, would find a way to do both, and do it smiling too. (He always did look good in photos.)

So, it was no surprise to me when, on the first day of music camp, it was him the wizened old man was looking for. I was late and was hurrying along a corridor of the music centre, shouldering my violin case, when I turned a corner and bumped into a wrinkled brown suit. With a small, old man in it.

I managed to keep my footing, but unfortunately, the old man did not have my acrobatic abilities of flailing around like a jellyfish.

'Hmph!' he commented, picking himself up off the floor and setting off again at a good pace in the same direction I was heading.

'Sorry,' I said, hugging my violin case and following him. No response. Was he angry with me? Only one way to find out—pester him some more and see if he minded.

'Why are you in such a hurry? Off to save the world?' I jested as we jogged along together.

He shot me a quick look. 'Very perceptive boy!' he praised. 'But we must hurry, or we will be too late!'

His joke was rather thin, but I laughed supportively anyway. Mum always did say I had to be polite and respectful to my elders.

We dashed down a few more corridors and finally arrived at the open concourse area of the music centre, where our school band instructor, Miss Rumi, had asked us to assemble. Most of the band kids were already there.

'Ah,' the old man said, rubbing his gnarled hands together, his white beard bobbing enthusiastically. 'Which one is Matthew Pane?'

I scanned the faces of the kids milling around but strangely, our blue-eyed boy was nowhere in sight. I looked at my watch. The time was 8.31 a.m. Matthew was officially late for music camp. Dread pooled in my stomach.

'He's ... dead,' I gasped.

'What? How do you know?' the old man demanded.

'Matthew is never late for anything,' I explained. 'Music camp starts at 8.30 a.m. and he's not here. That could only mean one thing.'

'That he's gone to the toilet?' the old man said hopefully.

The ear-splintering crash of a mobile phone hitting the hard concrete floor of the concourse area interrupted our conversation. We turned to see Miss Rumi standing all in a tremble among the electronic ruins. 'Matthew … is … dead,' she said in a quivering voice. 'Hit by lightning while on his way here …'

The entire concourse area fell into a stunned silence.

Then the students started screaming, and it was as if an orchestra had just started up. Miss Rumi did tell us that the acoustics of the place was excellent. I was just about to add my voice to the symphony when I noticed the old man's face. It was frozen in an expression of the deepest horror, and his fingers were clutching at his hair in an appalling disregard for the possibility that he might pull out those last few strands on his balding head.

I controlled my own feelings of shock and tried to console the old man. 'You've had a scare, Grandpa. Maybe you should sit down.'

At the sound of my voice, he turned away from the concourse area and looked at me—really looked at me, for the first time. 'Who are you?' he asked suspiciously.

'I'm Julian Kee.'

'And how old are you?'

'Um … thirteen?' I answered somewhat hesitantly, not sure where he was going with all the questions.

He looked me up and down, walked round me to study me better, then faced me again, stroking his beard. 'He will do, yes, yes, so he will,' he muttered to himself.

'Excuse me?' I asked.

He suddenly brightened, smoothed down his bushy white eyebrows with his two forefingers, then rubbed his hands in glee.

'Would you like to go undercover, wear cool clothes, fight bad guys, and save the world, though no one will ever know you did it?'

'You mean … like a spy?' I asked sarcastically.

'Exactly like a spy,' he agreed enthusiastically, pleased I had caught on so quickly.

'Uh … no,' I said, backing away warily.

'Okay, no cool clothes,' he said, as if *that* was the main impediment in an otherwise attractive job offer. 'I don't have the budget anyway. So, shake on it?'

'No!' I repeated, ignoring the hand he had stuck out for me to shake.

The man stopped grinning and peered at me curiously with his beady old eyes. 'Why not?' he asked. He seemed genuinely surprised.

'For one, I have no idea who you are.'

'That is true,' he said, 'though it is obvious enough that I'm a wise old man.' Here, he stroked his white beard pointedly. 'A mentor, some might call me, but, carry on.'

By this point, it was very clear to me that the old man was crazy (maybe from suffering a concussion when I had knocked him down accidentally), but I decided to humour him for just a bit longer. This, of course, is not what a sensible kid would do, but I guess I wasn't thinking properly, what with everything that had just happened.

So, I carried on. 'For another, I'm not "chosen one" material. I'm really quite mediocre. You were looking for Matthew, weren't you? Now *he* definitely fits the "chosen one" part.' Glancing at the chaotic scene on the concourse, I corrected myself: '*Fitted.*' Some students were crying while others seemed simply shell-shocked.

'Might you not be an orphan whose parents died under mysterious circumstances?' the old man asked hopefully.

'No, that was Matthew. I happen to have two parents, still very much alive.'

'Ah,' the old man said regretfully. 'But I bet there was always something different about you. Some misunderstood talent, like you can talk to snakes, maybe?'

'Nope. Afraid of all animals, even bunnies.' I paused, remembering how I had once run screaming out of my friend's house to escape his pet rabbit, and added empathically, '*Especially* bunnies.'

The old man was starting to look gloomy as he tossed out his next idea. 'Then you must at least be a loner. Nobody understands you because you're so brilliant!'

I felt bad for the old man. He was so clearly barking up the wrong tree. 'I failed my last mathematics test, actually. And also, I have two best friends,' I said almost apologetically.

'Two sidekicks!' He cheered up considerably. 'That's an awfully great advantage! Would one of them happen to be a spirit animal? No? Ah. That's a pity, but we'll make do.'

'I haven't agreed to whatever it is you're thinking of getting me to do!' I protested while trying to inch away without him noticing.

He noticed. 'You think I'm loony, don't you?' he said sourly.

Loony *and* creepy, I thought. 'Uh … my parents said I should not talk to strangers,' I mumbled lamely, realizing it was rather too late for that.

'All right!' the old man said, throwing his hands up into the air in exasperation. 'Go on! Live your petty little life, and don't cry when you are dead, because you soon will be, and everyone around you too, all because you didn't want to fulfil your destiny as the chosen one.'

'You didn't even come here to look for me. You were looking for Matthew,' I pointed out.

'Okay, listen,' said the old man in a conciliatory tone. 'I know you don't believe me, and who can blame you? But I can prove what I'm saying is true. I'll tell you three things that are going to happen. When you see that all my predictions have come true by tomorrow morning, you'll believe me then.'

'Okay,' I said doubtfully. I was thinking I could just listen to his crazy talk, pretend to believe him, then walk away and never see him again.

'First prediction: people will die by lightning today.'

I rolled my eyes. 'That's not a prediction. That's an observation. Matthew Pane just died.'

'No,' the old man interrupted. 'Matthew was just the tip of the ice cream—'

'Iceberg,' I corrected him.

'What? Oh yeah, I forget that you say things differently here. Where I am from—'

'Where *are* you from?' I cut in, suddenly suspicious.

'Ah,' the old man said with a mischievous twinkle in his eye, 'that's a secret you will only get to know if you agree to the quest. Now, back to the predictions.' His manner turned serious. 'So, there will be many deaths by lightning today, all around the world. Watch the news tonight. Second prediction: by the time you wake up tomorrow morning, dozens of hurricanes will have formed in the oceans and will be hurtling towards land. Third prediction: volcanoes that have been dormant for thousands of years will awaken, and your world will start to burn.'

I stared at the old man in shock. His words might have been the delirium of a lunatic, but the way he said it—so solemn and grave—could it really be true? Could our world be heading towards a disaster—no, a catastrophe—on a scale never before experienced? He said our world would burn …

'Wait a minute,' I said slowly. 'You said "your world will start to burn", not "our world". Where *are* you from?'

He gave me an enigmatic smile. 'I knew I wasn't wrong about you. Tomorrow morning, all will be revealed ... if you choose to come.' With that, he turned on his heel and walked off.

'Wait!' I called. 'If what you say is true, will tomorrow be too late?'

'There's nothing you can do to stop the three predictions,' he said without looking back or slowing down his stride. 'But you can stop what comes after. See how you feel tomorrow. If you believe me then, meet me back here, same time, same place.'

The old man walked away while I stood there, dumbfounded, trying to make sense of what I had just heard.

Three predictions; three disasters. After which, our world would burn. Where was the old man from? Could he really be believed? The way he said it, he sounded like he did not belong to this world. Had I been talking to an alien? Was I in danger of catching some alien bacteria? Was I going mad? Otherwise, why would I be asking myself so many questions in my head?

***

I walked into the concourse area where most of the band kids were still huddled, and found my two good friends, Mia and Ryan. Mia was trying to scare Ryan with a loud 'Hah!' in an attempt to cure his hiccups, which had apparently come on due to the shock of hearing about the Matthew incident. As for Mia herself, the whole sky had to collapse for her to be fazed.

'Who were you talking to? Hic!' Ryan asked.

'Some loony,' I replied, not bothering to tell them the full details of what had transpired. It was simply too crazy to be true.

It was a sad day at the camp. Miss Rumi was devastated as she had meant for Matthew to play the flute solo. All of us were in various states of grief too. The brass section was in particular trouble, as their tears kept getting into their instruments and they had trouble drying them out. It was a relief when the day ended and we were finally dismissed.

By the time I got home, I had convinced myself the old man was just some crazy doomsayer. How many people in the past had claimed to know the future and predicted the end of the world? Too many, that's for sure. And if we listened to them all and lived in constant fear of our imminent deaths—why, we wouldn't have bought such a comfortable sofa to sit on (as I plonked myself down on it), or such an elegant coffee table to put our feet up (as I leant back and raised my feet with a satisfied sigh), or such an expensive wide-screen TV to watch our movies (as I clicked the remote control).

And oh my goodness, the news was on, and everywhere in the world people were dying.

CHAPTER TWO

For the next twelve hours, I felt as if I was living in Nostradamus's paradise. First, all around the world, the air crackled nonstop with flashes of lightning. People dropped dead like electrocuted flies. Then, satellites everywhere started capturing images of gigantic hurricanes forming in all the four oceans. Ships capsized or were swept away by the wild, merciless winds that were even now racing towards the various coasts of the Pacific, Atlantic, Indian, and Arctic continents. By early morning the next day, mountains were venting ash and gas, and tremors could be felt within a few miles of any known volcano.

The world was ending, just like the old man had predicted.

The world was ending, and it was up to me to fix it. I sat on my bed in my room, hugging myself to still my trembling. Why me, of all people? Other than the fact that I happened to know Matthew, I could not understand why I had been chosen. After all, there was nothing special about me. I was just a normal thirteen-year-old boy with average height, average looks, and the average amount of nose hair. I didn't even wear spectacles.

I did, however, have two good friends, who would surely stand by me through thick and thin, and this thought buoyed me up somewhat, until I considered what I knew of my friends, and then my heart sank again.

First, Mia Pendrago, a stocky, broad-shouldered girl with thick wrists who played the drums in our band. Her mother was Chinese and her father English, and this dual heritage filled her with grandiose delusions. Half the time, she thought she was the reincarnation of King Arthur—he of the knights and round table; and the other half that of Qin Shi Huang—the first emperor of a unified China. It was perfectly acceptable to me that my friend should believe in the concept of rebirth though I did not subscribe to it myself, but when I asked her why she might not be the reincarnation of a Qing dynasty chamber pot scrubber, she could not explain and got angry with me instead.

My other friend was the thin and undersized Ryan Chowdhury, who lost his favourite stuffed toy when he was five—an incident that gave him the impression early in life that the world was a huge Venus flytrap that would swallow up everything that meant anything to him. As a result, he was careful never to show any outward joy for fear of tempting fate, and grew up a nervous, anxious boy, paranoid about anything that moved. He didn't play any instrument, being only interested in reading up on the theory but not in practising it, though I must admit he was very handy with arranging the chairs for our band performances.

What a ragtag team we would make, I thought despondently.

Miss Rumi had given us a holiday today to recover from the shock of Matthew's death, but I texted Mia and

Ryan to meet me at the music centre anyway. It took me a while to decide between the words 'urgently important' and 'importantly urgent', but finally, I was done and went out of my room.

My parents were on the sofa, their eyes glued to the TV and the footage of carnage all around the world. Although, to be more accurate, other than the lightning strikes and shipwrecks, the real damage was yet to come, for the hurricanes and volcanoes were only still brewing.

'I'm off to meet Mia and Ryan,' I said.

Mum turned around. 'Be careful,' she said solemnly. 'Stay away from volcanoes.'

'There are no volcanoes in Singapore, Mum,' I reminded her.

'Keep out of the paths of hurricanes,' Dad added in an equally serious tone.

I gave an exasperated sigh. 'We don't get hurricanes on our island. We're protected on all sides by Indonesia and Malaysia.'

Mum looked like she might mention the lightning strikes next, of which we got quite a fair bit in equatorial Singapore, so I hurriedly said my goodbyes and left.

***

Mia, Ryan and I met up at the music centre half an hour before the old man was due to arrive, and I quickly shared with them what he had said to me the day before.

'Swords in stones!' Mia exclaimed, once I had finished telling my story. Mia liked to curse in the way she imagined people did during the medieval times of King Arthur and Qin Shi Huang. 'So the old man spoke the truth after all!'

'We're all going to die,' Ryan said miserably.

'Well, supposedly I'm to save us all,' I reminded him, whereupon he gave a wail and said with even more conviction: 'WE'RE ALL GOING TO DIE!'

Mia patted Ryan on the back as if offering her condolences, while I gave him a withering look. 'Thanks for the confidence,' I muttered.

'Where and when did the old man say to meet him today?' Mia asked.

'Here and now,' a boisterous voice announced, 'although, I object to being called "old". Where I'm from, I'm in the prime of my life!'

I turned round and saw the old man from yesterday walking towards us. He was holding a plate in one hand and eating from it with the other.

'Just having my breakfast,' he said. 'Green eggs and ham, anybody?'

'No, thank you,' we said, our faces twisting into looks of disgust at the vomit-inducing food.

'Why not?' he asked in surprise. 'Dr Seuss said it's quite good. Always trust a doctor!'

'Er … Dr Seuss is not a real doctor,' Ryan said. 'He's a children's author, and he meant it as a joke.'

'Really?' the old man said in dismay. 'Eww.' He put the plate behind his back, then took out a white handkerchief to wipe his lips. Mia actually went round him to see where the plate had gone, but she looked back at us and shrugged. The plate had simply vanished.

'Grandpa, where exactly are you from?' I asked.

The old man tucked the handkerchief back into his pocket and looked at us. 'We had better sit down,' he said. 'It's a long story.'

There were some study tables with benches nearby, and we quickly settled ourselves down at one of the tables.

'My name is Wuchiwark,' said the old man when we were comfortably seated, 'and I come from the Underworld.'

What sort of a name is Wuchiwark? I wondered, then noticed that Ryan had gasped and was hunched up on his bench. I looked at him, puzzled. The name was odd but it wasn't *that* odd. Then my brain (which I admit works just a tad slower than Ryan's) moved on to the second part of Wuchiwark's sentence, and I too gasped.

'Are you a ghost?' Mia asked in wonder.

'What? Of course not!' Wuchiwark said, looking offended.

'An undead?' Mia pursued. Ryan whimpered and shrank further down into his seat.

'No!'

'But you're from the Underworld,' Mia said, looking confused.

'Yes, as opposed to the Overworld,' Wuchiwark said, as if that explained everything. And then, he did explain everything.

'You've all heard the idiom, "The world is your coconut",' he began.

'Oyster,' I corrected him.

'Ah yes. That's what you know it as. But what does it mean?'

Ryan raised his hand timidly. 'It means you have the opportunity to do anything you want.'

'Ah, but does it make sense?' Wuchiwark asked, stroking his eyebrows while watching us intently.

I had to admit it did not. This was one idiom I could never quite wrap my mind around. An oyster was small and enclosed by a shell. If the world was an oyster, wouldn't it be a very small world? Why should that mean endless opportunities?

'That is because the idiom that you know is actually a corruption of the original saying,' Wuchiwark said.

'Which is, "The world is your coconut"?' Mia asked.

'That is correct.'

'How is that any better?' I asked, feeling as if I were a foreign language student in an elementary English class on a bad day.

'You see,' the old man said patiently. 'The world is shaped like a coconut.'

'Or an orange,' Mia said. 'Or an onion. Anything round would work.'

'No, it has to be a coconut,' Wuchiwark said, 'for a coconut has a hollow in the centre. You see, the world that you know exists on the surface of the earth. That's the Overworld. But under the crust of the earth, there is another surface that people live on, too. That is the Underworld. Hence the saying, "The world is your coconut".'

My two friends and I exchanged looks.

He is really bonkers, Mia's look said.

Certifiably insane, Ryan's look added.

We should run, my face suggested. *At the count of three.*

Agreed.

Agreed.

I nodded, barely perceptibly, three times to indicate the count, then grabbed my bag and sprang away from the table at the same time that Mia said, 'How awesome!' and Ryan said, 'Cool!'

They both looked at me in surprise. 'What are you up to, Ju?' Mia asked.

'Uh, cockroach under the table,' I mumbled and sidled back to my bench, shamefaced. *Some sidekicks I had*, I thought resentfully.

'Go on, Grandpa Wuchiwark,' Mia urged.

'Well, the Underworld is very similar to the Overworld. We have soil under our feet, the sky above our heads. But because our environment is enclosed, we are safe from a lot of the natural dangers that you people face. We have no strong winds, no harmful radiation from the atmosphere, no extreme temperatures.'

'Where do you get your light from?' Ryan asked. All traces of his earlier timidity were gone now as he became engrossed in the intellectual discussion.

'Why, the sun, of course.'

'The sun shines through the earth's crust?' Mia asked doubtfully.

'No, we have our own sun. Do you know what is at the centre of the earth?'

'The core, a super-hot ball of iron that gives us our magnetic field,' Ryan said. It occurred to me then that now that Matthew Pane was no longer in the running, Ryan would be winning all the academic prizes our school had to offer. He was the smartest person I knew, other than Matthew. In fact, if this were a detective novel, and Matthew had died under more mysterious circumstances, Ryan would be a prime suspect for Matthew's death; he had the most to gain from it. But fortunately, this is not that kind of story.

'What you know as the core—that is our sun,' Wuchiwark said.

'What about night? Do you have night time?' Mia asked.

'Sure we do, any time we want it!'

'But how?' Mia asked.

'Oh, it's a simple piece of magic to black out all our windows so we have complete darkness whenever we want to sleep.'

Magic? The three of us exchanged looks again, although this time I did not try to interpret them.

Wuchiwark nodded. 'Oh yes, we Underworlders use magic all the time. It's easy to use, and environment-friendly too.'

'So Underworlders and Overworlders have always existed side by side, and we never knew?' I asked rather sceptically.

'Oh no. All life began in the Underworld. No one lived in the Overworld until a thousand years ago, when early explorers discovered natural fissures in the earth's crust that led up to this place. With the help of magic, we learnt about the dangers of your environment, and decided that while it would not be prudent for us to move our community up here, it would be the ideal place to banish our prisoners—not all of them, of course, but only those who had committed the most heinous crimes like murder, blackmail and drinking too much coffee.'

Ryan brightened at the chance to display the prodigious knowledge that had hitherto been collecting dust in his enormous brain. 'That's exactly like how England sent their prisoners to Australia in the nineteenth century, and how Korea sent theirs to Jeju Island during the Joseon Dynasty!'

Wuchiwark sniffed, 'Where did you think they got the idea? Copycats.'

'So we're all descendants of murderers, blackmailers and coffee addicts?' I asked, thinking, *that explains a lot.*

'That's right,' Wuchiwark said, nodding. 'However, we stopped banishing prisoners about two centuries ago, when your industrial revolution took off. We guessed where it would lead, and we were right—massive deforestation, global warming, nuclear warfare, extinction of quaggas … It was deemed too inhumane to send even the most vicious and maleficent criminal to this festering pit of human corruption.'

'Thanks a lot,' I muttered.

'What are quaggas?' Mia asked curiously.

'They looked like zebras,' Ryan volunteered the information eagerly, 'except they had stripes only on the front half of their bodies.'

'Correct,' old man Wuchiwark praised. 'So we closed up the fissures, wiped your memories of the Underworld, planted some fake dinosaur bones and other stuff in your soil to create a false history for your people, and henceforth cut off all our ties with the Overworld.'

'Dinosaurs are fake?' Mia asked, looking distressed. She loved dinosaurs.

Wuchiwark nodded.

'What about woolly mammoths?' she demanded.

'Fake.'

'Stonehenge?'

'Ho ho … we had quite a bit of fun with that—moving the gigantic stones into a random pattern with our magic and watching you people try to decipher some ancient meaning from it. Fake.'

'Qin Shi Huang?'

'Fake.'

'King Arthur?' Mia asked desperately. She was perspiring now, her face pale with dread.

'Our most nefarious criminal ever banished. Real.'

Mia heaved a big sigh of relief. Her identity was safe. She did not seem to have heard the 'nefarious criminal' part and I was in no hurry to point it out to her. Neither was Ryan, I noticed.

'But what has all this got to do with our current situation?' I asked, hoping to distract Mia. It worked.

'You said we had to save the world?' she added.

The old man nodded sagely. 'Our magic told us the Overworld is due for a massive disaster, on a scale so huge that it would mean total annihilation for your entire race. It would mean an apocalypse. Armageddon. Cataclysm. Decimation …'

'Um,' Ryan interjected. He was sitting next to Wuchiwark and was peering into his lap under the table. 'You can stop reading from your thesaurus now. We get the idea.'

Wuchiwark looked disappointed at the interruption as he put away his thesaurus in the same place that he kept his plate of green eggs and ham, and continued with his story. 'The cats held meeting after meeting on this issue, and finally decided that the Underworld would not interfere. We would let the Overworld destroy itself and everyone in it.'

'The cats?' I couldn't help thinking I had misheard.

'The C-A-T-T-S-S, pronounced "cats",' Wuchiwark clarified. 'Council for Analysing and Thinking Through Serious Stuff. It is made up of ten individuals and forms the ruling council of the Underworld. I am one of the ten, or was, until two days ago. I had tried to persuade my fellow council members that it would be too cruel to let billions of people die in the Overworld when we had the power to save them, but alas, my efforts were in vain.'

Putting on a pompous look, he moved a hand about as he intoned, as if addressing a formal audience, 'Why waste our magic on them? Let them be wiped out. Then we'll have a clean slate. We can start to send our prisoners there again.'

Wuchiwark shook his head and sighed. Resuming his normal voice, he said, 'That was what Miaowi, one of the leading councillors, told us. The other councillors said nothing to refute his argument. Finally, two days ago, I got so fed up with their idiocy that I resigned from the council. I decided that if they refused to do anything about it, *I* would. All the fissures leading to the Overworld were supposed to have been sealed centuries ago, but I knew there was one left open, in case of emergencies.

That particular tunnel was chosen because it opened up into one of the few places in your world that is fortunate enough to be protected from all major natural disasters by its geography—Singapore. So I secretly made my way here to find the hero destined to save your world.'

Ryan, Mia and I exchanged looks. We seriously should stop doing that since we obviously could not tell what those looks were supposed to mean.

'And what makes you think it's me?' I questioned.

'Because of the prophecy, of course,' Wuchiwark said.

'What prophecy?' I asked, curious.

'The prophecy that says Matthew—I mean, you, Julian Kee, will save the world.'

CHAPTER THREE

It must be true then! I had doubted my own capabilities, consumed with fear that I was not good enough. But if it had been prophesied that I too, and not just Matthew, was destined to save the world, then it must be true! I felt the warm blood of courage flowing in my veins, the plentiful calcium of strength straightening my spine. I sat up taller. Confidence flooded my cells, grit filled my heart—

'Can we hear the prophecy?' Ryan asked, interrupting my rousing internal monologue.

'Sure!' Wuchiwark said cheerily. 'I always carry it around with me so that I can refer to it when the time comes.' He reached into an inner pocket of his jacket and took out a slip of paper that had been folded several times. Opening it, he cleared his throat, then recited in a voice several tones lower than his usual:

'When the mountains weep blood,
And the sky explodes with light,

When the winds bring seas to land—
One brave boy will have the might,
And two sidekicks along him fight,
To thwart the heavens' evil plan.

His number of years is unlucky,
But his land of birth is not.
This boy will find the hidden key,
In the form of a glowing rock.
And his name, his glorious name,
Is the one and only Matthew Pane.'

'Jousting knights!' Mia gasped. 'Matthew Pane? Didn't he die yesterday?'

In an instant, all my newfound confidence and heroic delusions evaporated. 'I knew it,' I said glumly. 'You were just trying to cheat me into believing I'm the chosen one. I've always known it was Matthew all along.'

'Wait!' Wuchiwark said hurriedly, in his normal voice. 'I haven't finished reading. There's one last stanza.' He then lowered his tone and continued:

But if this Pane has come to grief,
There's always a Plan B:
Another boy can take his place—
His name is Julian Kee.'

'There!' he said triumphantly, looking up.

'I've never heard a prophecy that was so specific,' Ryan said doubtfully. 'Usually, it's full of riddles and nobody really understands it until the end of the book.'

'My dear boy, this is real life, not a book!' Wuchiwark said, shaking his head disapprovingly.

'Let me have a look at that prophecy,' I said, snatching over the slip of paper before Wuchiwark could object.

'Give it back!' he cried, clawing at the paper. Mia twisted the old man's arms behind his back while I laid the paper down on the table so we could all see it. Printed in the elegant, antique font of Bookman Old Style were the first two stanzas of the prophecy. Beneath those lines, scrawled untidily in blue ink, was the last stanza. There were even a few cancellations, with the replacement words written above the crossed-out ones.

'You only just wrote the last stanza yourself, after what happened yesterday!' I accused.

'And you didn't even bother making up six lines, like the original two stanzas,' Ryan pointed out sadly.

The old man massaged his arms, which Mia had just released. 'What does it matter?' he asked, sounding somewhat exasperated. 'The fact is that your world is dying, and I can tell you how to save it. Do you want to do it or not?'

'We need some time to talk it over among ourselves,' I said. 'It's a big decision. We don't want to rush it.'

'Fine,' Wuchiwark said. 'I'll give you five minutes.'

He stood up and walked away from us, then sat down on the steps leading down to the outdoor area of the concourse.

'What's he doing?' Ryan whispered.

Wuchiwark had taken out a small, spiral-bound notebook and a pen. He opened the notebook, then gazed into the distance while tapping his pen against his chin. He appeared to be deep in thought.

We watched him for a moment, then Mia gave a sudden gasp. 'Clanking amours! I think he's composing a new stanza to the prophecy! Ju, if you don't agree to take up the quest, he'll give it to someone else!'

'And good riddance to it!' I said heartily.

'Do you really mean that, Ju?' Mia asked.

'I have always found it odd that even when I am very sure about something, I will immediately become unsure once someone asks me that,' I remarked, stalling for time. This was a life-changing decision. Surely I deserved a minute or two, or maybe a year, to think about it.

But Mia took my words as a signal that I was getting persuaded, and she beamed at me and made small circular motions with her hand as encouragement for me to carry on.

'I don't know,' I said slowly, trying to figure out exactly how I felt about the whole affair. 'I mean, it was very flattering when I thought I could be the hero to save the world, but the prophecy wasn't even meant for me. It was for Matthew! *He* would have done a great job. I'll probably just mess things up.'

Mia scrunched up her face, then put one stout foot on the bench and both fists against her waist. I groaned inwardly. Whenever she got that look, I knew I was in for a lecture. 'Matthew is dead, Julian,' she said firmly. 'Get used to it. The fact is that *you* were there when Wuchiwark was looking for someone to take over. This *is* your destiny. Our world is going to burn, and you can stop it. Don't you want to do something meaningful, for once in your life?'

I decided to gloss over the insult in her last sentence and focus on the more positive aspects of her speech. 'I guess the chance to be a hero doesn't come every day,' I acknowledged.

Ryan, who had been listening quietly, said tremulously, 'But it'll be very dangerous, won't it? "Thwart the heavens' evil plan",' he read from the piece of paper. 'You'll have to go against some supernatural power. How will you stop volcanoes from exploding and hurricanes from blowing? It's impossible, Ju. It's a fool's errand. A death warrant. A one-way trip!' And he said all that without recourse to a thesaurus too.

'Oh, Ryan,' Mia said testily, 'don't ruin it for all of us. This is Julian's destiny, and who knows, it could be mine too! I'm not the reincarnation of King Arthur for nothing, you know. I'm meant for something *big*. I know it, I just know it!'

I looked at Mia. She seemed on the verge of tears, and her face was set in an attitude of stubbornness and determination. It occurred then to me that in considering this whole business, I had been selfishly thinking only about myself. Mia wanted— no, needed—to go on this adventure, and she could go only if I did. 'All right, Mia,' I said softly. 'Let's do it.'

Her face lit up. 'Really?'

I thought again about how even when I was very confident about something, I would immediately become unsure once someone asked me that. But something told me Mia's reaction would be less encouraging (to put it mildly) if I voiced it out this time. So, I threw away caution (and my better judgement) and committed myself with a nod instead.

Ryan groaned. 'Can I not go?' he pleaded.

'You don't have to if you don't want to,' I said generously.

'No!' Mia said. 'You have to! The prophecy says "two sidekicks". If you don't go, it may ruin our chances of success!'

I was beginning to think that maybe Mia would benefit from my ruminations about selfishness when Wuchiwark ambled over to our table.

'So, what's the conclusion?' he asked cheerily. 'We are wasting time, my friends!'

Mia and I turned to Ryan, who looked like a muffin cornered by a hungry child. After several heart-stopping seconds, when we could see him visibly struggling with his thoughts, he gave a timid nod. Mia's shoulders relaxed in relief.

'We're in,' I announced to Wuchiwark and immediately thought of following that up with 'and ... we're out' but somehow found the inner strength to keep that second part to myself.

'Oh well, there's a good rhyme wasted,' he said under his breath, tearing out a page from his notebook and ripping it to pieces. 'All right!' he said to us. 'Now that you are committed, I will share with you what you need to do. The clue is in the second stanza.' He read out:

> *'His number of years is unlucky,*
> *But his land of birth is not.*
> *This boy will find the hidden key,*
> *In the form of a glowing rock ...'*

'Er ... the rest of it is not relevant. As you can see, the prophecy mentions a thirteen-year-old boy—thirteen being commonly seen as an unlucky number, as I'm sure you know. He's from a lucky land—that's Singapore, a place of no natural disasters. It is he who will find the hidden key.'

'Why a thirteen-year-old?' I asked. 'Won't an adult be more capable and have more resources?'

Wuchiwark shook his head. 'Adults are not so good at this sort of thing. Their minds are less gulli—I mean, more rigid, and they are less able to accept realities that conflict with what they have believed all along.'

Mia tapped impatiently at the piece of paper. 'Tell us more about this key.'

'The key refers to the glowing rock, known in the Underworld as the Ef-frock. It is the source of all the magic in the Underworld. With this rock, we'll be able to stop the volcanoes and hurricanes from destroying your world.'

'Why is it called an Ef-frock?' Ryan wanted to know.

'Its original name was Ever Rock, meaning it has always been around, since anyone could remember. But try saying Ever Rock ten times, each time faster than before. Go on, I'll wait.'

Ryan took up the challenge. 'Ever Rock, ever-rock, everock, everock, effrock ...'

'Oh!' we all said.

'So, how does the rock work?' Mia asked.

'Just get the rock and bring it to me. I will activate the magic,' Wuchiwark said, puffing out his chest and thumping it proudly. Then the air went out of him, and he shifted in his seat uneasily. 'Er ... I might as well tell you now that the rock might not be very willing to go with you.'

'Huh?' I asked eloquently.

'Yeah ... and it has a bit of a temper too,' the old man said, almost sheepishly.

'A badly behaved rock?' Mia said with scorn. 'I won't give it a choice whether to come with us or not!' She brandished her powerful, drum-beating fists.

The old man brightened. 'That's the spirit. I knew I could count on you kids. Now, there isn't much time. You must go to the Underworld and bring the Ef-frock back to me by this evening. I will be waiting here for you at 7 p.m.'

'Do you have a mobile phone?' I asked. 'Can we call you if we encounter any difficulties?'

'Do I have a what?' Wuchiwark asked.

'Mobile phone,' Ryan said, taking his out to show the old man.

Wuchiwark looked scandalized. 'Your long-distance communicating devices won't work in the Underworld!

Technology is the bane of all existence. Haven't you kids been listening?'

'Your lack of technology is going to be the bane of our existence,' Mia muttered.

'They all speak English down below?' Ryan asked, ever the practical boy.

'Of course. Once, we spoke many languages, but as the prophecy came into prominence, people gradually leant towards English, since it is the language the prophecy chose to come in. Everyone feels they ought to be prepared for the day the hero comes.'

'Can't you come with us?' Mia asked anxiously.

'I would love to, but I can't,' the old man said with a sigh. 'Because of my insistence on saving the Overworld, I was branded as an outlaw the moment I left CATTSS. My face is too well known in the Underworld. I will not be able to take two steps before I'm arrested. Fortunately, I was able to leave the Underworld via the secret entrance before the notice of my criminal status went out to the guards.'

'So they know you're in the Overworld? Will they be able to find you here?' I asked.

'Only if I'm foolish enough to stay in the same place for more than half an hour at a time,' Wuchiwark said, waving a hand dismissively. 'They can use their magic to track my aura, but I need to be in one place for more than half an hour before my accumulated aura will be strong enough for them to detect me.'

'Um, Grandpa Wuchiwark,' Ryan said, looking at his watch, 'I think we've been talking to you for twenty-seven minutes.'

The old man jumped up in fright and started trembling all over. 'Is that right? I have to go!'

'Wait, you haven't told us how to get to the Underworld and where the rock is!' Mia cried.

'The secret entrance is in the grounds of the Botanic Gardens,' Wuchiwark said, talking very fast. 'Look for the swans. They'll show you where to go.'

He glanced nervously at his watch. 'Twenty-eight minutes!' he exclaimed, shaking even harder and talking even faster than before. 'Once you're in the Underground, go to the citadel. Be careful! There will be people with orders to kill any intruders.' He started to walk away, then suddenly turned back. 'I nearly forgot to give you these. Here, good luck!' He had drawn out a handful of colourful paper and thrown them on the table.

'What are they?' I asked.

He was already walking away rapidly. 'Stickers!' he called out without turning around. 'Use them wisely! They are muff muff mumble mumble …'

'What?' I asked, chasing after him. 'I couldn't catch your last few words!'

'Muff muff mumble …' the old man said as he rushed down a corridor.

I hurried down the corridor as fast as I could, but when I reached the corner, the old man was gone. There was nothing I could do but trudge back to my friends and tell them the bad news.

'You could have turned the corner and caught up with him!' Mia cried.

I stood dumbfounded for a moment. 'Yeah, I didn't think of that,' I said at last.

Mia shook her head in exasperation. Meanwhile, Ryan was examining the stickers. They were rectangular and flat, and each about the size of my big toe. (And unlike most other authors, I will provide the helpful information that my big toe measures 3 cm in width and 5 cm in length, so that you can accurately picture the size of the sticker. You're welcome.)

There was an assortment of pictures, and each picture was paired with a different number. The sticker with the number ten, for example, had a drawing of ten parrots. The number three sticker had a picture of three sunflowers. These stickers with their numbers and corresponding pictures were obviously a toddler's counting cards.

'Old man Wuchiwark thinks we're still little kids, bribing us with stickers!' Mia complained. She grabbed a handful and dumped them into a nearby trash bin. She was about to sweep up the rest when I stopped her.

'Wait—they're quite cute,' I said, bending down to pick up a couple that had fallen on the floor. 'We could give them to Ryan's little sister.'

'Aw, Mia,' Ryan complained as he sorted through the remaining stickers. 'We don't have a complete set now.'

I peered into the trash bin. The discarded stickers were lying on some rotten banana skins and half-eaten packets of noodles. 'Ew, gross,' I muttered, quickly abandoning my intention of retrieving the stickers.

Ryan had finished looking through the handful of stickers left and passed Mia one. It had the number nine and a picture of nine cookies. 'You might as well throw that away. It's a duplicate.'

'Sure,' Mia said, taking the sticker and tossing it into the bin. '*Now* can we get going?' she asked impatiently. 'We only have one day to find the Ef-frock and bring it back.'

Ryan hurriedly stacked the remaining stickers and stuffed them into his jeans pocket.

'The Botanic Gardens?' I asked.

'Right,' Mia replied, then added, a bit too cheerily in my opinion, 'We're off to save the world!'

CHAPTER FOUR

We got off the train at the Botanic Gardens station and entered the north-western side of the gardens through the ornate Bukit Timah gate. All three of us had been to the Botanic Gardens at least once before, but always guided by family members or teachers, and none of us had taken the pains to remember the layout of the place. Now, staring at the map erected strategically at the entrance, we realized with dismay that we had not thought this through.

Wuchiwark had said to look for swans. The map showed the locations of the three lakes in the gardens: Eco-Lake, Symphony Lake and Swan Lake, spread out in different parts of the sprawling gardens. 'Now, where would be the most likely place to encounter swans here?' I wondered, scratching my chin. It was impossible to guess.

'Um … *Swan* Lake?' Ryan said, helpfully emphasizing the word 'Swan'.

'Why are we looking for swans anyway?' Mia asked. 'How are swans going to show us the way?'

'There's a swan sculpture at Swan Lake,' Ryan replied. 'Maybe what Wuchiwark meant was that the secret entrance to the Underworld can be found there.'

'That must be it!' Mia said. 'Let's go!'

'Did anyone hear Wuchiwark mention there will be people trying to kill us?' Ryan asked nervously.

'No,' I said.

'Neither did I,' Mia concurred.

We would have taken a bus from the music centre to the Tanglin Gate entrance on the southeastern side of the Botanic Gardens if we had planned this out earlier, but it was too late for regrets now, so the three of us began the long walk to the other end. Fortunately, it was still only early morning and a cloudy day besides, so it was quite a pleasant walk and probably very good for our constitutions, except that we were all stressing out over the dangers that were lying in wait for us on our quest.

Since our cross-gardens trek took us past Eco-Lake and Symphony Lake, we were able to confirm there were no swans in those lakes, which made us more confident that Ryan's conjecture must be correct. Indeed, half an hour later, when Swan Lake came into view, we saw that in the centre of the small lake was a bronze sculpture of five swans, their wings outspread and their necks craning forward, frozen in the process of taking flight from a ruffled base of bronze reeds.

Two real swans idled nearby, their white feathers pristine against the greenish lake waters. They swam up to us when they saw us coming down the lane and made gentle honking noises. Visitors often fed the swans and fishes here even though doing so was illegal, and the swans were clearly expecting us to give them food. Mia shooed them away impatiently while I hid behind her. Animals freaked me out. Who knew what murderous intent lay behind those innocent-looking eyes?

For all we knew, the unintelligible sounds animals made to each other were secret communications with the aim to exterminate all mankind. Eventually, the two swans wizened to the fact that we did not carry treats on us, and swam indolently away.

Finally, we were left alone to examine the sculpture. The problem was that it stood in the middle of the lake, which made it impossible for us to get up close to it, and we could only look at it from about a good ten metres away. The bronze swans were of monstrous size, at least several times that of a real swan. There could be any number of places on the sculpture that might serve as buttons or levers, and the base of the sculpture was certainly large enough to contain a hidden entrance.

'What should we do?' Ryan asked, looking around us fearfully. There was no one in sight, however. We were safe, at least for the moment.

'It has to be that sculpture,' Mia said. 'What else could it be?'

'So we have to swim over?' Ryan asked doubtfully. 'I can't imagine Wuchiwark emerging from the Underworld and getting himself all drenched.'

'The sculpture doesn't look very old either,' I added. 'Not likely that an age-old secret entrance has been built into it. Maybe the entrance is near the sculpture, not in the sculpture itself?'

'I think you're right!' Ryan said, looking surprised that I could come up with such a good idea. 'Wuchiwark said the swans will tell us where to go. Look! All five of them are facing the same direction. Maybe they're pointing in the direction of the entrance!'

We followed the path circling the lake to reach the opposite side, which only took us about a minute as the so-called lake was really nothing more than a small man-made pond. We searched among the pebbles, reeds and bushes, but could not figure out what the birds were pointing at, if anything.

'Time is running out,' I said in frustration. 'We only have until seven tonight to report back to Wuchiwark, and it's already half past ten!'

'The swans will show us, the swans will show us,' Mia grumbled. 'I don't see any swans showing us anything! We'll never get into the Underworld at this rate. Great lot of help they are, these swans.'

'Hey, don't you blame us for everything,' one of the white swans protested.

'That's right,' said the other, who had a slightly yellowish neck. 'How were we to know you're looking for the Underworld if you didn't say so earlier?'

'Yikes!' Ryan shrieked, jumping behind Mia.

'Yikes!' I echoed, darting behind Ryan and holding on to his shoulders. He was shaking so violently that I couldn't tell if I was trembling too or if it was all just him.

'Talking swans!' Mia said in a reverential tone.

It seemed that while we were rooting in the grass for the entrance, the two real swans had swum up to us unnoticed and were now waddling up the grassy bank. They opened their wings and shook the water from their bodies, then tucked their wings back comfortably and fixed us with glassy stares.

'They must be mechanical,' Ryan whispered to us from behind Mia's back.

'We're not mechanical,' the yellowish-neck swan declared loudly. Sounding hurt, he turned to his companion: 'Why would they think we're mechanical?'

'Because they're spies from the Overworld, Ovid!' the pure-white swan hissed. 'That's why they don't know animals from the Underworld can talk!'

'But Horace, they knew about the Underworld,' Ovid said. 'And they knew we could show them the way. We heard them!'

'It's too suspicious. They're spies, I say!'

'Maybe we should question them. We could use torture!'

'I say we kill them right away.'

'Ahem,' Mia cleared her throat conspicuously. 'We can hear everything you're saying, you know.'

The two swans stopped their discussion abruptly and turned towards us simultaneously, hooting most ferociously and flapping their wings. Only then did we see the arsenal of daggers and shurikens glinting from under their feathers.

The swans' eyes flashed with malice and I knew I had only seconds to think of a foolproof plan to evade this crisis. It had to be flawless; any error could result in the three of us being decorated with dagger hilts and pointy ends of shurikens.

So I peeked out cautiously from behind Ryan and stuttered, 'Don't … don't kill us. We're friendly.'

Mia sighed at my lame words and I gulped. After all, there really was no reason for them to believe me. I ducked my head back behind Ryan and prepared myself for imminent annihilation by swans.

To my surprise, the swans stopped their advance. 'You are?' the swan named Horace asked, cocking his head.

Encouraged, I stuck out my head again. 'Yes!' I said, injecting more enthusiasm into my voice. 'We were invited to visit the Underworld. Why else would we know about it?'

'I told you!' Ovid said triumphantly to his partner.

Horace scratched his head with a wing. 'But why didn't the CATTSS tell us?'

'They probably did,' Ovid said, looking sheepish.

Horace sighed. 'I wish you hadn't eaten that memo.'

'They shouldn't have hidden it in a cookie,' Ovid lamented bitterly. 'You know I can never resist a cookie.'

'Well, now we have no idea what instructions the CATTSS gave us. We should have requested for a resend.'

'And get me sacked?' Ovid asked resentfully.

'Of course not, but it sure makes our job very confusing now.'

'Um,' Mia dared to interrupt the killer swans' tête-à-tête once again, 'we're still here.'

'Right,' Horace said, raising his head in a dignified manner. 'Tourists to the Underworld, are you?'

'Yes,' I said eagerly. 'As stated in the memo, you know.'

'See? They even know about the memo!' Ovid said in relief.

'Everything's all right then,' Horace said officiously. 'Come on, we'll show you the way.'

Ryan, Mia and I walked behind the waddling swans as they led us down the path fringing the lake. The silence was a little awkward, so Mia tried to break it with a cheerful, 'So, why did the CATTSS choose you two, of all people—I mean animals— to guard this very important entrance?'

'Shh!' I told her, afraid the swans would be offended and start waving their weapons about again.

Fortunately, the swans did not seem to have heard her, as they were poking around the ground with their beaks. In fact, they appeared to be nibbling on some grass, occasionally dipping their heads in the lake—in short, doing normal swan stuff. They seemed to have forgotten all about us.

'Hey,' Mia called to them. They continued on their own swanish business and ignored us.

'Talk to us,' she said, then more loudly when they did not respond, 'talk to us!'

Just then, a man and a woman strolled by holding hands. They must have been walking behind us for some time without us noticing them. 'Such strange kids,' the woman commented to her partner, giving us a sideways glance. I waited till their backs were to us before sticking out my tongue at them. The couple walked to the far end of the lake and followed the lane deeper into the Botanic Gardens. It was only when they had disappeared from view that the swans hopped back on to the path.

'Right,' Horace said briskly. 'Follow us.' He nosed under a rock for a bit, and suddenly, a grass-covered trapdoor opened up in the ground right next to the path. Peering into the hole, we saw what looked like the top of a very long slide.

'In you go,' Ovid said.

'Wait a minute,' Horace said. 'What about the protocol?'

'Oh yes, the protocol,' Ovid said. 'It's been so long since we let in tourists that I forgot all about it!'

'What protocol?' Ryan asked anxiously.

'Oh, you just swear to a bunch of stuff, nothing much really,' Horace said reassuringly. 'Go ahead, Ovid. Fire away.'

Ovid puffed his chest out self-importantly.

What would he make us swear to? For the first time since agreeing to go on this mission, I seriously considered what I had got myself and my friends into. Would I have to make promises that would force me to betray every shred of honour I had, forsake every scrap of morality I had grown up with, and abandon every value I held dear? Fear trickled down my forehead in the form of little beads of sweat.

Ovid finally spoke. 'First, do you solemnly swear to never reveal the secret of this entrance to anyone?'

He was starting us off easy. 'Sure, we can promise that,' I said with great confidence.

Ovid carried on: 'Second, do you swear to guard any knowledge you gain of the Underworld with your life?'

Ah, the questions were getting harder. But of course, we had already known it would not do to go around blabbing about the world being a coconut and not an oyster. After a quick exchange of glances, we agreed to this too, albeit with some hesitation about the 'with your life' part.

'Finally, do you swear not to eat the cookies in the pantry down below, without permission, no matter how hungry you are?'

'Wait a minute, that's not in the protocol,' Horace interrupted.

'Those cookies belong to us!' Ovid hissed. 'It's part of our benefits package. I'm not letting some tramp eat them up!'

'But what if we are near starvation and will die if we don't get a bite of cookie?' I protested. I knew the questions would get harder but I didn't think they would get this hard.

'Dents on shields! Just promise them, Ju,' Mia hissed at me under her breath. 'We need to get moving or we'll be too late to … you know what.'

I looked wretchedly at my friends. I had never felt more torn in my life. Cookies or saving the world? It was an impossible choice to make.

Fortunately, the decision was taken out of my hands as Mia ran out of patience and bravely cried out, 'I promise!' and stepped on the slide. In a moment, she was whizzing down the chute and her cry of 'Whee!' echoed back up the tunnel. Ryan was trembling with fear, but to his credit, he too quickly promised and followed Mia into the hole. I had no choice but to mumble my agreement and leap in after my two sidekicks into the deep, dark void.

CHAPTER FIVE

It was a very well-constructed slide, angled steeply enough for a smooth descent, but not so steep as to be frightening. Air vents carved into the sides of the tunnel provided ventilation, and though we were shrouded in darkness, it was a comfortable ride. I found myself relaxing, the anxieties of the past few hours melting away. Eventually, I even fell asleep.

After some minutes, I was jolted awake when I emerged from the slide. The weird thing was, the slide actually came from the ground, and I was shot into the air like a marshmallow and came to a gentle rest on a very comfortable mattress. I was still marvelling at how gravity worked in the two worlds, where down in one world was up in the other, when Ryan and Mia pulled me off the mattress and to my feet.

'Wasn't that cool?' Mia gushed. 'World's longest slide ever!'

'We should find our way out,' Ryan said nervously. 'The sooner we finish our mission, the better!'

I nodded, but couldn't help lingering to admire the rather pleasant lounge room we were in. Watercolour paintings of forests and lakes hung on the walls. There were several cushions scattered about the plush carpet floor, and against one wall was a low cabinet. A glass jar filled with chocolate-chip cookies stood upon it. On the opposite wall, a flight of stairs led up to a round trapdoor in the ceiling.

'So this is the swans' pantry,' I remarked. 'Cushy job they have!'

'Well, our job is less cushy, so we had better get moving,' Ryan said firmly.

'All right,' I sighed.

I led the way up the stairs, popped open the trapdoor, and found myself in the typical opening scene of a student's composition. The sky above me was an azure blue and the grassy plains that stretched out in all directions from me were a verdant green. Birds chirped in unison all around me, and the gentle sun was a benign presence on this beautiful, autumnal day.

Ryan and Mia had followed me above ground and were looking about them with equal pleasure. I took a few steps on the wonderful carpet of green, then could not resist sitting myself down so that I could touch with my bare hands this softer-than-down bed. The grass looked dewy but did not feel wet, and the soil beneath it was dry but not hard, so I was perfectly comfortable without dirtying the seat of my jeans. Instinctively I knew, even without looking, that in this paradise there would be no ants or ticks or indeed any other annoying insects that I would have to worry about. I lay down gazing at the sky rapturously with my head cushioned in my palms.

And immediately received on my face a wet blob of bird poo.

The culprit was long gone by the time I was upright, and I found myself shaking my fist at a black speck that soon disappeared in the distance.

'Aw, Ju, that's bad luck,' Ryan said sympathetically and Mia patted my shoulder.

Heroes should not be wishing for their mothers when they are on a quest, but I could not help thinking wistfully that if my mother were here, she would straightaway whip out a packet of wet wipes and hand a piece to me. As it was, I had to grab a handful of grass and try to clean myself as best as I could.

'That's not going to get you very clean,' a cheerful voice piped up from somewhere near us.

Ryan literally jumped at that unexpected sound, and Mia leapt into a defensive stance with her right hand ready to deliver a karate chop. The only weapon I had was the poo-stained grass, so I prepared to flick it at the enemy.

But when we looked up, we saw that the person walking towards us was only a young girl. She looked about the same age as us and had the most pleasant, open-hearted face. Her fair hair was pulled up on both sides and tied at the back, with the rest of her long hair left draping down. She wore a white blouse tucked into high-waisted dark brown pants. Sand-coloured boots that zipped halfway up her calves completed her outfit.

'Why don't you use a sticker?' the strange girl suggested.

'Good idea,' I said and Ryan took out the small pile of stickers Wuchiwark had given us. I took the topmost piece and proceeded to wipe my face with it. I don't know why I had thought it would be a good idea, because paper didn't clean my face any better than grass did, and it was such a small piece besides.

The girl looked horrified. 'That's not how you use stickers!' she exclaimed.

'Pasting it on my face is not going to clean it any better either,' I said, annoyed, throwing the stained sticker on the ground and wiping my hand on the seat of my jeans. By then,

I had smeared bird poo all over my face and was in a very bad humour.

'Why not?' she asked. 'Here, let me see.' She sifted through the pile in Ryan's hands and chose the sticker with the number two. 'This should do for a small job like this.' Before I could protest, she had peeled off the backing and pasted the sticker on my forehead. Keeping a finger on the sticker, she said, 'Make bird poo and acne disappear.'

Immediately, I felt as if the skin on my face had tightened and a soothing sensation settled over it.

'Your face!' Mia said, startled.

'What? What?' I asked anxiously.

'The poo is gone, and your pimples too!'

I swept my fingers over my face. It felt as smooth as a baby's, except for the part that had the sticker plastered on it. I peeled away the sticker and noticed that its colour had bleached to a pale off-white. 'How did you do that?' I asked the strange girl in amazement.

'Cleaning up the poo is such a small job, I didn't want to waste the magic in the sticker, so I added in the acne,' the strange girl said with a shrug.

Magic? Ryan, Mia and I stared at the stickers in a mixture of awe and dismay. 'So that's what they are for. And we threw most of them away!' I said with regret. Guiltily, I bent down and picked up the poo-stained sticker I had discarded earlier and put it into my jeans pocket.

'I can't believe magic really exists!' Ryan gushed. I could almost see the contents of his overstocked brain moving around to make space for this new piece of information.

'Hello ... talking swans?' Mia reminded him.

'You're obviously not from here,' the girl said. 'Just arrived from the Overworld, have you?'

'Yes,' I said, recovering my composure. 'We're tourists from the Overworld.'

The girl frowned. 'Since when did the CATTSS allow tourists?'

'Since they sent the swans the memo,' I replied without missing a beat. I had said this often enough now that I could do it with a straight face and a very negligible amount of snickering.

She looked uncertainly at us for a moment, during which I tried to stifle my giggles. Ryan chewed his fingernails nervously, while Mia readied her karate hand chop behind her back. Then the girl broke out in a brilliant smile. 'Nobody could get past the formidable guardian swans unless they allowed it, so you must be right. Welcome to the Underworld! My name is Karina.'

Everyone relaxed. 'I'm Julian, this is Ryan and that's Mia,' I said.

She looked at each of us, delighted. 'You're the first tourists to the Underworld in ages! Can I be your tour guide? Please, please?'

'Well …' I said, feeling conflicted. On the one hand, we were on a secret mission, but on the other, we probably needed some local help if we were to survive in this unknown land.

'We need some local help if we are to survive in this unknown land,' Ryan whispered to me.

'That's right,' Karina chirped. 'And I'm happy to help.'

I made a mental note to tell Ryan later that his whispers were way too loud. Still, his views accorded with mine, and I was leaning towards allowing Karina into our gang when I felt Mia plucking at my sleeve. When I turned to look at her, her face was screwed up in an attitude of pique. 'The prophecy said two sidekicks, not three!' she hissed into my ear. 'Taking her along might just mess with the outcome!'

'What prophecy?' Karina asked cheerily.

I made a second note to tell Mia to tone down her whispers too.

Or maybe I should just tell them to quit whispering altogether. I sighed. Was there no end to the work I had to do? Being a leader was a more tiresome job than I had anticipated.

I turned back to Karina and was about to assure her that there was no prophecy when she recited:

'When the mountains weep blood,
And the sky explodes with light,
When the winds bring seas to land—
One brave boy will have the might,
And two sidekicks along him fight,
To thwart the heavens' evil plan.'

'That the one?' she asked cheerfully.

We stared at her, open-mouthed and wide-eyed.

'How … how did you know?' Ryan stammered.

'The Ef-frock has only ever revealed one prophecy and everyone in the Underworld knows it! There's even a tune written for it.' She began to sing the words of the prophecy to a slow, mournful melody that brought tears to my eyes.

'Stop it, this is too sad,' Ryan sobbed.

Karina obligingly stopped mid-song and said, 'Which of you is Matthew Pane? Oh, I wish I'd brought my autograph book. This is such a glorious moment!'

'Um, Matthew is dead,' I confessed. 'I'm his replacement.'

'Dead!' Karina's hands shot to her mouth. 'Those are big shoes you're stepping into, Julian!'

'I know,' I admitted. 'I'm not much, compared to Matthew, but we three are the Overworld's only hope now.'

'And since you know the prophecy,' Mia snapped, 'you should understand why you can't join us. Ju can't have three sidekicks.'

'Oh, I won't be a sidekick,' Karina said. 'I'll be a guide. No problem at all!'

'Fantastic!' I said, pleased that she had found such an elegant solution, and shook her hand. 'Welcome on board!'

Ryan seemed satisfied, though Mia still looked unhappy. 'Don't blame me if things go wrong because of *her*!' she said in a fierce whisper.

'Oh, it won't go wrong because of me,' Karina said cheerily. 'If anything goes wrong, it'll more likely be because of that!' She pointed at the grass some five metres away from us, and I gasped. Metal spikes each the width of my forearm (measuring 7 cm in diameter) and spaced about the length of my thumb (also 7 cm—in length, not diameter) apart were rising up rapidly from the ground all around us!

Ryan and I were too stunned to react, but Mia made a lunge for the bars. Unfortunately, even Mia's quick reflexes were too slow and she could not get out in time. When the bars were about one and a half times my height (I'm 1.6 m tall. You're welcome, again), they started to curve inwards until they met at the centre of the circle. We were now entirely trapped within a metal cage.

'Oh no,' Ryan cried, running to the metal bars and shaking them. 'They won't bulge!'

Even Mia's thick, strong drummer's arms could not dislodge the bars. 'Try using a sticker!' she suggested.

Karina shook her head. 'It won't work. This kind of mechanism is created using high magic, which cannot be undone by stickers. The CATTSS must have placed it here as an automatic defence against intruders from the Overworld.' She paused, narrowing her eyes at me. 'Which makes it very clear, you're not tourists after all. There was no memo!'

'The CATTSS don't approve of us trying to save the Overworld,' I admitted.

'And how were you planning to do that?' Karina asked.

'This ex-councillor from CATTSS called Wuchiwark told us to steal the Ef-frock.'

'Wuchiwark? He … he told you to steal the Ef-frock?' Karina echoed, colour draining from her face.

'I suppose now you won't want to help us any more,' Ryan said gloomily.

Karina stood undecided for a moment. We watched, fascinated, as her expression went through a series of changes: fear, then anger, then wonderment, and finally settling on a happy, satisfied look.

'Internal struggles over?' Mia asked sarcastically.

'Yes!' Karina replied, not seeming to have picked up on Mia's scorn. 'I'm with you on this. It's a noble cause, and well worth risking life and limb!'

'You really think we'll have to risk life and limb?' Ryan asked pathetically.

'Oh yes!' Karina said happily. 'No doubt about it!'

Ryan started to tremble, and I knew I had to get the gang moving before he had a total mental collapse. Besides, with my natural leadership instincts, I knew that standing in a cage was not very good for the team's morale.

'We need to find a way out of here,' I reminded them.

'What about the swans' pantry?' Mia asked suddenly. 'It can't be too far away. I think it's within the cage!'

'Yes! Let's go back into the lounge and discuss our options,' I agreed. Fortunately, I had not closed the trapdoor, so we found the hole with no difficulty when I fell into it accidentally, and the rest climbed back down into the room as well.

'The activation of the cage will bring the CATTSS' lackeys here,' Karina warned us.

'How long will they take?' I wondered, rubbing my bruised bottom.

'If they use a Level Ten sticker to teleport, they'll be here in five minutes,' Karina said.

'The greater the number, the more powerful the sticker?' Ryan asked.

Karina nodded. Ryan gave Mia a glum look. 'You threw away a Level Ten sticker!' he lamented.

'You asked me to throw away a Level Nine one!' she countered.

'It's all right,' I hurried to interject, before they could begin quarrelling for real. 'It's the fault of the noodles and banana peel,' I added, cleverly deflecting the blame from either of them, and also to assuage my guilt for not picking up the stickers from the trash bin.

'You guys are weird,' Karina commented. 'Anyway, I doubt the CATTSS will waste expensive Level Ten stickers just to check who has been caught in the cage. After all, they expect your retreat to be cut off by the guardian swans so you can't escape. No one has ever been able to defeat the swans before, so they won't worry about you getting away. I reckon they'll take their time to get here.'

Something didn't seem right to me, and I tried to put it into words, with great success: 'But if we managed to get into the Underworld and activate the cage, that means we are able to get past the swans. Won't the CATTSS realize that?'

Karina stared at me. 'You're right! They'll be here any minute then. We have to get out now!'

'We know that,' Mia snapped. 'But how?'

CHAPTER SIX

Mia and I both looked at Ryan, who gulped and then quickly set his big brain to work.

'We could see if there's a chainsaw here that we could use to cut the bars,' he suggested. We obligingly searched the room, but nope, no chainsaw.

'We could dig under the cage with a shovel,' he said next.

'Can you stop thinking of ideas that need equipment?' Mia asked, looking as if she wanted to strangle Ryan in exasperation. 'Isn't it obvious this room has nothing of that sort?'

'We could persuade them to believe we are tourists,' I said hopefully.

'The people who set this cage trap will know there was no such memo!' Ryan objected.

After five minutes of discussing various strategies, it gradually became clear to Ryan, Mia and me that the most attractive option was to get on to the slide, return to the Overworld, and tell Ovid and Horace that we were finished with our travels. But if we did that, there would be no stopping the natural disasters that would soon be devastating our world. Could we really be so selfish? Could we still live with ourselves, knowing that our cowardice had doomed everyone to a horrible death? We were just beginning to conclude that we could, when we heard a crunching sound coming from a corner of the room. We all turned towards the sound and saw that Karina had opened the cookie jar and was munching on a cookie.

'You're not supposed to eat that!' Ryan exclaimed in horror.

'That's right! You'd better stop now and give me the rest of the cookie!' I added, salivating.

'Says who?' Karina said, taking another bite.

'The swans made us swear not to!' Mia growled. 'Now you're going to get us into trouble with them too!'

Karina shrugged. '*I* didn't swear. If I'm going to be on the run from the CATTSS, I need to keep my energy up.' Her jaws moved again, then abruptly stopped. Her face tightened in a grimace. 'Ew. The chef didn't mix the batter properly.' She put her fingers into her mouth and pulled out a small, crumpled piece of paper. 'Oh!' she said, looking at it in surprise.

'What's that?' I asked eagerly.

Karina smoothed out the slip on her palm and read: 'As mentioned in our previous memo, we have set up a cage trap in case the outlaw Wuchiwark returns. However, should the cage be accidentally activated, you may switch off the mechanism by pressing the button under the cookie jar. Signed, Miaowi, CATTSS Councillor.'

Mia quickly lifted the cookie jar and indeed, there was a large, round button embedded in the cabinet top. I pressed it, and we could hear a mechanical hum that lasted about ten seconds. When the sound had died down, the three of us Overworlders whooped and exchanged high fives.

'You saved us!' I told Karina gratefully. 'You're an awesome tour guide!'

Karina blushed. 'It's nothing. We'd better get out of here though. The CATTSS might still send someone down to check what went wrong.'

We hurried back up into the open and indeed the cage was gone. I closed the trapdoor, which, once shut, blended in with the rest of the field so well that we would be hard-pressed to find it again. Karina saved the day once more by taking a Level Three sticker from us and saying, 'Show us back to this exact spot when we want to leave the Underworld.' Mia kept that sticker in her pocket, so it would not be mixed up with the rest.

That settled, I looked around us. The plains stretched out far and wide in all directions, and I realized we had no idea where to go to find the citadel that supposedly housed the Ef-frock.

Fortunately, our tour guide again had some answers for us. 'The Ef-frock is hidden deep in the CATTSS fortress, known as the citadel,' she told us. 'I can show you the way, but first, you need a change of clothes, otherwise you'll stand out too much. Also, you'll need some equipment. My uncle-in-law's cousin's step-daughter's sworn brother owns an outfitter's shop. And because I'm such close relatives with him, we can totally trust him. Let's go there first.'

Glad to have someone tell us what to do in these dark, uncertain times, we gamely trotted along with our new friend as she led us across the plains and then deep into a grim, menacing wood.

Trees with thick, green foliage crowded in on us, resembling the tropical forests I was used to in Singapore's nature parks. There was no boardwalk here, however, nor any clearly defined dirt path. Still, Karina advanced through the wood in an assured manner, no trace of hesitation in her steps.

I'd never enjoyed walking in nature parks, since animals had the annoying habit of appearing when you least expected them. Fortunately, the good thing about forests in the Underworld is that you get all the joys of nature without having to worry about wild boars or bees or banana-snatching macaque monkeys. When I remarked on this to Karina, she explained, 'Animals here respect human boundaries. They would never think to intrude into our personal space.'

'Not even when they're starving and a yummy-looking human walks by?' Ryan wanted extra reassurance.

'But they're never starving,' Karina said. 'Why would they be? There's food everywhere.'

Indeed, here, deeper into the woods, the trees were bursting with delicacies of every kind. Apples, oranges, cherries, roast beef, steamed eggs, ice cream—you name it, they have it.

'I've never seen a roast beef tree before,' I said mildly, not wanting to draw too much attention to my ignorance.

'Neither have I,' Karina said frankly. 'Whatever you feel like eating, the trees of the Golden Forest will provide. You must be hungry. Go on, help yourself.'

Now that she mentioned it, I remembered I had not eaten anything since breakfast, and it was about lunchtime. I broke off a slice of roast beef from a branch and took a bite, while Ryan and Mia watched me anxiously. When I did not drop dead, they too helped themselves to the fried chicken and burritos conveniently located on some low-hanging branches.

When I had eaten my fill, I remarked, 'A drink would be nice,' and sure enough, I soon spotted some cup-shaped flowers hanging off a branch. A sip of their cool contents assured me I would not die of thirst in the Golden Forest.

As we walked, Karina explained to us the business with the stickers. 'They're issued by the CATTSS,' she said. 'The councillors extract magic of varying potencies from the Ef-frock and put them into stickers, labelled one to ten according to their levels. They are then distributed among the populace according to a fixed quota. They're very valuable and can be used as currency too.'

'What about magical artefacts like that cage that nearly trapped us?' Ryan asked. 'Do they have stickers pasted on them to make them work?'

'Sometimes,' Karina replied. 'But often, those artefacts already have the magic leached into them, so they can function without a sticker pasted on them all the time.'

'How would you make such an artefact?' he asked eagerly, whipping out a notebook and pen from his pocket, all ready to take notes.

'You can't,' Karina laughed. 'You have to attend a special college to learn how to do that. Some of the councillors have been trained, since they need to know how to extract the magic of the Ef-frock into stickers. Also, some very enterprising businessmen, like my relative, Botuni, have invested years of their lives learning this skill so they can have an edge over their competitors with their magical wares. Look, we're here.'

Sprouting out of the ground in the middle of the forest like a gigantic mushroom was a cottage covered with ivy. A jovial, middle-aged man with grey hair fringing a bald pate was standing in the doorway and he waved at us as we approached. 'No point wasting magic on hair!' he said cheerfully when he noticed Mia staring.

'Botuni, we're going on a quest and need some stuff,' Karina told him.

'No problem at all,' Botuni said. 'Not up to some trouble, are you?' He eyed us shrewdly. 'Does your father know?' he said to Karina.

She made a face. 'You won't tell, will you?'

'I won't if you don't want me to. After all, you're my very own sworn brother's stepmother's cousin's niece-in-law. All right, what do you need?' Botuni brought us into his cottage, which was basically an enormous storeroom. Shelves lined each wall from floor to ceiling, and every shelf was overflowing with things.

'You got new stuff!' Karina exclaimed and went over to a corner to admire some equipment she had not seen previously.

'Going on a quest, are you?' Botuni said to the rest of us. 'I've got everything you could possibly need. See here? This bottle contains tiny crystals that will turn into pillows when you pour them out. Very useful when you need a good night's sleep. And this tube contains a cream that will cure writer's block. Just rub a small amount on your forehead and the elusive words will come, though the quality of writing is not guaranteed. And on this shelf—'

'Botuni,' Karina interrupted, coming back to us. 'We need the real adventuring stuff.'

Her relative's face fell. 'But I just acquired this—a ball of fluff that can turn into any stuffed toy you want, even limited editions of Hello—'

'Botuni,' Karina said again, her face stern.

The outfitter sighed. 'All right, all right. What do you need?'

Karina thought for a bit. 'I'm not sure. All I know is that we will definitely have to navigate a maze or two.'

'Ah,' said Botuni, shaking his head. 'That's the one thing I cannot help you with. A maze is a maze. You just have to find your own way.'

'I know of some maze-solving strategies we could try,' Ryan piped up, his colour rising upon hearing of an intellectual challenge. 'Always turning left at every turn, marking the walls with arrows, using a string—'

'Oh look!' I interrupted excitedly. 'Nail clippers! That could be useful. Wait a minute, these look second-hand ...'

We spent some time rummaging among Botuni's gear. He was not allowed to sell stickers, as they were all CATTSS-issued and strictly regulated, but he did show us lots of other useful stuff, and by the end of half an hour, we had each taken our pick. Karina also helped us choose clothing and shoes that were similar to hers. My loose, long-sleeved white shirt had cross strings tied in front, which made me look very stylish in a medieval way.

'How are we going to carry all this?' Mia asked, staring at the huge pile of loot we had stacked on a table.

'You'll put them in backpacks, of course,' Botuni said, handing each of us one that was about the size of my head (which was about 55 cm in circumference).

'It's too small,' Mia complained. I hoped she was talking about her backpack, not my head.

'No, it's not,' Botuni said indignantly. 'This is a standard-issue adventurer's backpack. Guaranteed to hold six items, no more, no less.'

'He's trying to con us into buying a lousy backpack,' Mia whispered to me and Ryan.

'A suspicious one, are you?' Botuni chuckled. 'Go on, try it.'

Mia picked up the six items that she had thought might come in handy on our quest. They fit just nicely into the backpack.

'See?' Botuni said, spreading his palms wide to emphasize his point.

With a triumphant twinkle in her eye, Mia said loudly, 'Hmm … I've changed my mind. I won't take this frying pan after all.' She reached into the bag and pulled out the large cooking implement. 'With the freed-up space, I'll put in five of these daggers instead.'

The odd thing was that after the first dagger had entered the backpack, the other four fell with four pings outside of it. The backpack was full to overflowing, with not even an empty nook to slot another dagger in. Mia stared at it in shock, I whistled in awe, and Ryan scribbled furiously in his notebook. The six-item rule indeed could not be breached. Mia had no choice but to return the frying pan and four daggers to the shelves.

After we were done packing our stuff, Botuni announced merrily that our purchases amounted to 'a paltry forty gold coins'. I pinched Karina's sleeve and pulled her aside. 'How are we going to pay for all this?' I whispered, and rather successfully too, for unlike my friends, I was perfectly capable of speaking quietly.

'Don't worry,' Karina said. 'I'll put them on my father's tab.'

'Won't he be angry when he finds out?'

'He buys so much stuff from Botuni that he probably won't notice an extra forty gold coins on his monthly bill.'

'Hmm … Will he notice fifty?' I asked. I had been happy with my white shirt but now was thinking about swapping it for the red and gold one with a matching crimson cloak that hung from a very handsome-looking mannequin that stood near the entrance of the cottage. A sword with an embroidered leather scabbard hung from its side. Funny I had not noticed that outfit earlier. It was exactly what I imagined I would wear if I were a hero on an adventure in a medieval world.

'What are you doing with this ragtag bunch, Karina?' the mannequin asked while giving me a once-over with its haughty, scornful eyes.

I jumped. A talking and moving mannequin? What new magic was this?

'It's none of your business, Tago,' Karina said coldly.

The boy named Tago, whom I had earlier mistaken for a handsome mannequin, said cloyingly, 'Your business is always my business, Karina. Don't you know that by now?'

'Go away,' Karina said rudely.

'I can go away, but I won't be gone forever,' Tago warned, the sweet tone disappearing from his voice. 'You're betrothed to me, and by all that is foul in the Overworld, I *will* have you as my wife once we come of age.'

'Not if a dragon eats you first,' Karina growled.

'Calm down, children,' Botuni said, moving to stand between them. 'It's still five more years before you turn eighteen. Lots of time to talk things over.'

'Or to train a dragon,' Karina muttered. 'Come on. Let's go.'

* * *

Karina strode out of the cottage so quickly, her backpack swaying with each angry step, that we had to hurry to catch up with her. She led us through the woods in silence, and she was so clearly in an ill temper that we did not dare to interrupt her thoughts with speech.

As I walked behind her, my mind was awash with countless questions. In the couple of hours that we had interacted with her, she had seemed so independent, so sure of herself. Who would have thought her future had been decided for her, against her wishes? What sort of person was this Tago anyway, to make her dislike him so intensely? When would we dare to ask Karina if she was just walking blindly or in the right direction towards the citadel? Where indeed, *was* the citadel? How long would it take us to get to it? Why didn't I add a majestic-looking cloak to my outfit while I still had the chance?

It was just as well that Karina decided to break out of her funk at this moment, as I was just about to run through another cycle of Who-What-When-Where-Why-How questions.

'Thank you,' she said when she turned to face us. Her face was slightly puffy and her eyes red, as if she had been crying.

'Um … you're welcome?' I said, not sure what she was thanking us for.

She took a deep breath. 'Tago is the son of Miaowi, a councillor of the CATTSS. We both live in the City of a Thousand Spires, and he has been after me to marry him ever since we met at a party years ago. Last year, in a bid to curry favour with Miaowi, my father agreed to betroth me to Tago. We are to be married when we turn eighteen. Most days, to avoid running into him, I will leave the city to wander around in the countryside. What a stroke of bad luck that he would visit Botuni today! Luckily I was with all of you and could stalk off with my pride intact. If I were all by myself, he would never have left me alone.'

'I'm so sorry,' I said, feeling genuinely bad for her. From my brief encounter with Tago, he struck me as a perfectly detestable person and certainly did not deserve a beautiful crimson cloak, not to mention a nice girl like Karina. I told her as much, and she laughed—a pleasing sound that made me think of rain falling lightly on a hot summer's day.

'We'll get you a cloak some day,' she promised, looking a lot more cheerful than before.

We started walking again, and I heard Mia whispering to Ryan behind us in an exaggerated, coquettish tone: 'Oh, poor me! I'm so rich, I'm so pretty, I have so many problems!'

I really must get round to talking to Mia about her whispering soon.

For now, all I could say was, 'Uh …' while looking awkwardly from Karina to Mia and back again. Ryan looked embarrassed as well and dug his elbow into Mia's side to shush her, but Mia just tossed her head defiantly.

'It's okay,' Karina said. 'I don't care what she thinks of me. She's going to be dragon food by the end of the day anyway.'

'You don't really mean that, right?' Ryan asked, a forced lightness in his tone.

'Don't I?' Karina said casually, then ignored him and Mia altogether as she walked shoulder to shoulder with me along the forest path.

It seemed that even in her earlier distress, Karina had been leading us the right way, for we soon emerged from the woods and were out in the wide plains again, except that this time, we could see in the far distance, shimmering slightly under the sun as if it were a mirage, the skyline of a city filled with countless spires and towers.

'Behold, the City of a Thousand Spires,' Karina announced, 'capital of the Underworld, headquarters of the Council for Analysing and Thinking Through Serious Stuff, and home to our source of magic, the one and only Ef-frock.'

CHAPTER SEVEN

'Are there really a thousand spires?' Ryan asked excitedly. 'Does every building have a spire? What happens if someone builds a new building? Will the city then be called City of a Thousand and One Spires?'

'Can we not be sidetracked again?' Mia said before Karina could reply. 'Let's quickly go and get the Ef-frock!'

'Okay,' I said excitedly, starting to walk towards that shiny city. I felt fearless, armed as I was now with a backpack full of useful adventuring stuff.

Karina stared at me as if my face had gone green and tiny snowmen were dancing on my head.

'You can't be thinking of walking all that distance!' she exclaimed.

'Why not?' I asked. 'It's just there.' And indeed, the city looked barely an hour's hike away.

She shook her head. 'The city only looks near because it's so huge. The thinnest of those spires is as wide as a three-lane carriage road. It'll take us the whole day to walk there.'

'We don't have a whole day,' Ryan said worriedly. 'We have to meet Wuchiwark at 7 p.m. today!'

'Precisely,' Karina said. 'Let me have a look at your stickers.'

Ryan pulled them out of her pocket and passed them to Karina. There were only two left. 'Are these all that you have?' she asked. 'Wuchiwark didn't give you more for such a dangerous quest? That stingy, old—'

Ryan had started to tremble upon hearing the word 'dangerous'.

'He did give us more,' I said with a sheepish glance at Mia, 'but we kind of … well, we lost some of them.'

Karina pursed her lips and sighed. 'I was hoping we could teleport there, but we don't have enough magic. We'll have to call some quaggas instead. They're slower than teleportation, but it still beats walking.'

'Quaggas?' Ryan asked eagerly, perking up. Even Mia could not hide her look of interest, although she had been steadfastly ignoring Karina all this while.

'Yes, faster than a cheetah and better stamina than a horse.'

'How do we call them?' I wondered aloud.

'With quagga food,' she said, passing the stickers back to Ryan. She took off her backpack and knelt on the ground. 'Good thing I took some from Botuni just now. I did think they would come in handy.'

She removed a packet of biscuits from her backpack and tore it open. Then she scattered the biscuits on the grass, taking care to cover a wide area, and crushed a few under her boots to release a unique smell, which, she explained to us, was a combination of grass, leaves, tree bark and quagga pee.

'Now what?' I asked.

'Now we wait,' she said.

'For how long?' I asked, worried that we would not get to the Ef-frock in time.

'What did you say?' Karina shouted, for a thundering noise had risen up and was making conversation difficult.

'I SAID,' I yelled, 'FOR HOW LONG?'

And was butted in my back. 'Stop it,' I said irritably, thinking it was Ryan or Mia playing the fool with me. I was butted again. 'Will you s—' I turned and immediately jumped back. 'Wha—!'

The most beautiful, elegant creature with a white body and black stripes on its front half was standing right in front of me. She was now grazing on the biscuits that I had been stepping on, and with her head bent, I could see that the black stripes extended up into her short, even mane.

Once I was done admiring the creature, I looked around and realized that a whole herd had arrived. At least twenty of them were nosing quietly in the grass, searching for the biscuits. The birds that had flown up in alarm when the quaggas had stampeded across the plains now settled back on their perches in the shrubbery, evidently fully at ease in the company of these gentle beasts.

'Quick, get up on one,' Karina instructed. 'Once they've eaten all the biscuits, they'll run away!'

Even though I was frightened of the creature, I was more overawed by the majestic steed and honoured that I would be able to ride one. I grabbed the mane of the white quagga that had butted me and swung my right leg over her, feeling very grand indeed. I was exactly like a shiny knight in the tales of old, albeit with no armour, no lance or sword, and as it turned out, no skill, for I promptly slid off the quagga on the other side when she gave a little shake.

'You have to introduce yourself first,' Karina said, sounding exasperated. She was already sitting astride a magnificent grey quagga. 'Don't you learn manners at all up in the Overworld?'

How does one speak to a quagga? Probably with great reverence and formality, I decided. And so I said, 'Hail, oh wonderful quagga. My humble name is Julian.'

The quagga looked up and stopped chewing. 'Hi, old chap! Nice to meet ya. I'm Squig. Come on up!'

I had forgotten that animals in the Underworld could talk. How very convenient! I thanked Squig heartily and clambered on to her back, then looked up to check how my friends were doing. I had expected Ryan to shy away in fear of the wild beasts, but to my surprise, he was already on his own brown quagga, and was chatting away happily with it. Mia had also chosen a brown quagga, but hers had white legs.

'Tell your quaggas where to go,' Karina said. 'If we get split up, meet under yonder bridge.'

'Yonder where?' I asked, but it was too late, for Karina was already speeding away on her steed. If she had been gesturing in a particular direction when she spoke, I had missed it as I was busy trying to figure out how to get a good handhold on Squig's mane. Oh well, I would cross that bridge (yonder bridge?) when I came to it.

'City of a Thousand Spires,' I told Squig, hoping to catch up with Karina. Squig took a final chomp, then kicked her heels and took off. If you have ever taken a bullet train, you will know what it feels like to be moving at an insanely improbable speed on the ground. Squig had never taken a bullet train, and so did not know that moving at twice the speed of a bullet train when you have a human on your back is not only insane but also maniacal, and should be made illegal. The scenery streaked by us so quickly that I could not even check to see if it was my life flashing before my eyes.

Fortunately, I did not die, and in no time at all (which was actually ten minutes, according to my watch), Squig came to a sudden halt a short distance from a well-maintained road that led to a very large and ornate gate. High walls stretched out on both sides of the gate, beyond which I could see gigantic steeples crowding into each other as they shot up into the sky. It looked as if a fairyland theme park designer had gone overboard and put in way too many towers.

'Goodbye,' Squig remarked and shook her rump, causing me to fall off and land painfully on my buttocks.

'Ow,' I groaned.

'If you ever have need of me again, say "ow" in exactly that tone,' Squig said. 'Other than a good sense of smell, we quaggas have excellent hearing too. Ta-ta!'

Mia and Ryan had also just arrived, and together, the three quaggas trotted back into the plains.

'That was amazing!' Ryan gushed, his face red with excitement. 'I learnt so much from my quagga! Did you know that animals here, including humans, live twice as long as they do in the Overworld? And that there are no four seasons here, only one—Just Nice? And did you know—'

'Any useful information on where to find the citadel?' Mia interrupted.

'I was just warming up to that question,' Ryan said, 'and then the journey ended.'

'Ryan!' Mia said, exasperated.

'Sorry, I didn't know we would get here so quickly.'

'It's okay,' I assured Ryan, secretly annoyed with myself for not thinking to see if Squig could give me any information that might help us in our quest. 'We don't want word to get out that we are looking for it. In fact, we don't want people to know we're from the Overworld. That's why I didn't talk to my quagga at all.' I looked around for our guide, but neither she nor her quagga was anywhere to be seen.

Mia looked irritated. 'Karina ditched us on purpose! I knew she was up to no good!'

I couldn't believe Karina would abandon us after all the help she had given us. There had to be a good reason why she was missing. Mia was just being prejudiced. She had objected to Karina joining our team from the very beginning and had been finding fault with her ever since. 'Come on,' I said to Mia in a stern tone, 'be fair. She's probably a much better quagga rider than you or Ryan and got here faster. At least *I* waited for you, didn't I? Come on, let's get into the city. Karina said to meet her at some bridge or other.'

Mia gave me a scathing look as if to ask which part of my brain was broken, but at least she quit complaining.

***

We took the road and walked towards the city gate, which, although wide open, was guarded by six burly-looking men attired in green-and-brown livery. They were all holding crooked wooden sticks that looked like tree branches but, in this magical world, could well be rods that would turn your insides into marshmallows.

Mia was eager to approach the gate, but Ryan stopped her.

'How do we get past the guards?' he asked nervously. 'I don't suppose they'll just let anyone say "hello" and walk in just like that.'

At that moment, a few men dressed like we were walked past. 'Hello!' they called to the guards, who smiled and stood aside for the men to walk in.

Ryan still looked scared. 'They're okay with adults, but what about kids? They'll probably wonder what a bunch of kids are doing by themselves, trying to get into a city without their parents.'

Just then, a group of teenagers who looked not much older than ourselves overtook us and reached the gate. They waved to the guards, who waved back cheerfully, and let them pass.

'Their world doesn't have as much crime as ours,' I reasoned, trying to psych myself up into feeling more confident, 'that's why they're quite lax in their security.'

'Their guards aren't as guarded,' Mia agreed. 'We should be able to get in without any problem. Everyone, look casual.'

The three of us sauntered up to the gate, trying to stem our inward trepidation with outward gaiety.

Although my heart was thumping wildly, I sang out a breezy 'Halloo!' to the guards, while Mia and Ryan gave them friendly waves. I hoped the guards assumed Ryan had naturally huge eyes instead of realizing they were actually wide with fear.

The guards smiled good-naturedly and waved us through. Heaving great sighs of relief, we stepped past them and into the wide passageway that led to the city proper. That was it! We had infiltrated the great City of a Thousand Spires! Wuchiwark had asked if I wanted to be a spy, and although he did not have a clothing budget, here I was nonetheless, with my two sidekicks, having acquired for ourselves the garb of an Underworlder, and we had with the help of our own wits and my not-inconsiderable charm, successfully made our way into the …

Out of the corner of my eye, I spotted one of the guards, a rough-looking man with an abundance of facial hair, whispering to another, who was totally bald. A second later, they both turned to look at us. Instinctively, feeling their gaze upon us, all three of us turned to look at them as well.

'It *is* them!' the hairy guard cried upon seeing our faces.

'Catch them!' the hairless guard shouted. He stood with his legs apart in a threatening pose and pointed his tree branch at us. 'Don't let them get away!'

'Run!' I yelled, and the three of us took to our heels.

'Why did you waste time standing there and saying "Don't let them get away?"' I heard the hairy guard berate his colleague as they started after us. 'We would have caught them already if we had run straightaway …'

The rest of his words were lost in the clamour of legs pounding on the ground as we raced down the passageway and reached the cobbled streets of the city. 'Which way?' Ryan gasped.

We had arrived at a crossroads, and all three choices available to us (the fourth being undesirable for the simple fact that it led back to the gate) looked identical to me. Each was flanked by similar rows of shops and houses, with people milling around the streets.

In such a situation, there were many ways we could have decided which path to take (the most scientific one being eeny meeny miny moe), but at that moment, shouts of 'Catch them!' reverberated behind us. I dared to throw a look behind my back and instantly regretted my supreme act of courage, for the sight of four muscular guards waving tree branches while running after us sent a shiver down my spine.

'No time to think!' Mia cried, and pulled me and Ryan towards the street directly ahead of us. 'Now will you believe that Karina has betrayed us?' she spat out as she ran.

I did not reply, for I was too busy running for my life.

CHAPTER EIGHT

We wove our way through a small crowd of townsfolk who were walking along the same cobblestone path. There was nowhere to go but forward as we were blocked on both sides of the path by the houses and shops. Gradually, the path turned so that once we rounded the bend, we were out of sight of our pursuers. Within a few seconds, however, they would surely turn the corner and catch sight of us.

I continued running forward but was jerked unceremoniously to a halt by Mia pulling on my sleeve. 'Here!' she cried, pointing to a doorway ahead that was slightly recessed into the building's walls. It turned out to be the entrance to a tavern, and we huddled in the doorway, panting, not daring to peek out.

In the space of mere heartbeats (and our hearts were beating really fast), the four guards ran past our hiding place and continued on the path, waving their tree branches and yelling as they went along.

'We should go,' Mia urged. 'They'll double back in a while when they realize we aren't in front.'

'I can't run any more,' Ryan whimpered, sitting down on the doorstep with a groan.

'Marauding dragons!' Mia cursed in exasperation. 'Show some courage, Ryan! Ju, can you make him—'

She trailed off as she realized why I had been so quiet. I was staring at the wall next to the doors of the tavern. A poster was pinned to the wooden slates of the wall, and smiling out at us were the faces of three remarkably good-looking criminals, namely, us.

'Wanted—dead or alive!' proclaimed the headline of the poster. Under our mug shots were the words, 'Spies from the Overworld! Reward for capture: three Level Five stickers.'

Ryan clapped his hands to his mouth as if to prevent himself from crying out.

'If ever I get my hands on that sneaky little—' Mia said, gnashing her teeth, then grimacing. 'Ow,' she said, holding her jaw, 'that hurt more than it would seem from books.'

'But why would she do this?' I said, bewildered. 'After helping us to escape the cage in the plains and getting us these clothes—'

'She didn't mean to help us escape the cage,' Mia said viciously. 'She only found the note because she was greedily eating the swans' cookies. And she brought us to Botuni as a delaying tactic. Maybe she contacted CATTSS from Botuni's cottage! Come to think of it, she walked away from us for a while when we were distracted by all the goodies Botuni was showing us.'

I must have looked really dejected because Mia said, 'Cheer up! We're not done for yet. Let's find the Ef-frock and then get our revenge on her for the betrayal.'

The soldiers' shouts, which had been growing more distant, were now becoming louder again. Their lack of discretion was really quite useful in alerting us to their whereabouts. One of them even hollered helpfully, 'They might be in that tavern doorway! Let's head over!'

We looked at each other in alarm. Ryan pulled himself together and pointed weakly at the tavern door. 'Do you think there's a back door through there?' he asked.

'Good idea,' I said.

We pushed through the swing doors and found ourselves in a large room. Scattered about the place were customers having their midday meal or simply enjoying a drink at the bar counter, which occupied a long stretch of wall across from where we stood. To the right and left of the counter were closed doors, leading to goodness knew where.

After a moment's hesitation, I pointed to the door on the left and we hurried over. Just as we were about to reach it, our view was blocked by a massive white apron. I stumbled backwards and looked up into the ruddy face of a rough-looking matron. She flared her nostrils as she glared at us and strands of black nose hair emerged from their caves and waved frantically for a second before retreating again. She put her swollen hands on her ample hips and intoned, 'And where do you young punks think you're going?'

'Um, nowhere,' I squeaked and backed away, bumping into Mia and Ryan, who were just behind me.

'No one gets into Mistress Malory's kitchen,' she warned us, brandishing a frying pan, which she had picked up from the counter. 'No one!'

'Ye … es, ma'am,' I stammered, wondering if by 'no one' she also meant 'no three'. I was just thinking of asking my friends when I noticed Mistress Malory was studying each of us in turn. 'Erm …' I said nervously.

Her expression turning mild, she leant forward and tucked the frying pan into her waistband behind her back. 'I'd let you in quietly for a sticker, though,' she said.

The shouts of the guards sounded as if they were just outside the tavern. I looked at my friends and they nodded. I hoped their nods meant 'we agree to give her the sticker' rather than 'we agree we shouldn't waste our stickers like that'. In any case, there was no time for clarification. So, using my prerogative as the de facto team leader, I said to Mistress Malory, 'We'll give it to you in the kitchen.'

'Follow me then,' she said with a wicked grin.

The kitchen was much cleaner than any I had ever seen in the Overworld. Pots and pans gleamed from various hooks, and the countertops were spotless. Soups were bubbling from stone stoves that did not seem to have any fire and the delicious smell of freshly baked bread wafted out from open shelves next to neatly stacked plates and bowls.

'Takes a great deal of magic to run a perfect kitchen,' Mistress Malory sniffed. 'I should ask you what you are running from, but I don't have that luxury. Ever since the CATTSS reduced the sticker quota, I can never get enough of them for my kitchen.' She showed us an empty palm, and Ryan dug into his pocket. He looked at the two stickers we had left, then passed her a Level One sticker with visible reluctance.

'Not very generous tippers, are you?' she remarked dryly. 'I could have offered you a concealed tunnel that leads out to the river, half a mile from here, but in exchange for that measly sticker, you'll have to get out from that back door over there instead.'

'A fair exchange,' I took the time to say before making a beeline for the door. It opened into another street similar to the one we had just left.

We heard the kitchen door open just as we slammed the back door shut behind us. Then Mistress Malory's voice boomed out: 'They tried to bribe me into silence but I wouldn't take it, loyal citizen of the Underworld that I am. They went through that door over there!'

'Surly jesters!' Mia cursed as we started running again. 'Is there no honour in this Underworld? *We* should be banishing *our* criminals down here instead!'

Within seconds, we heard the tavern's back door slam open against the wall. Glancing back as I ran, I saw the hairless guard standing at the doorway, the other three jostling behind him. 'There they are!' he bellowed, swishing his branch at us menacingly. 'Stop, I command you!'

'You can talk as you run, you know,' the hairy guard said, pushing his colleague forward, and soon, we had all four guards on our heels again. This street, perhaps because it was a back one, was way less crowded than the one we had just left. In fact, after we passed a woman carrying a basket of laundry, we found ourselves all alone on the long, cobblestone street that was gently sloping upwards. In a short while, our thighs began to ache from the uphill climb. Curses coming from behind assured us that the guards were similarly feeling the pain.

'There are no innocent bystanders we might hurt here,' the hairy guard panted to his comrades. 'It's time to use some magic! Are you ready?' He paused dramatically, then shouted, 'Release the Krake-rope!'

Wha—?

The tree branches from three of the guards flew towards us, and in an instant, they had resolved into sinewy shapes like the tentacles of some mythical sea monster. They curled round our bodies, tightening with every struggle we made and binding our arms against our torsos. The Krake-ropes lengthened as they wound round us, and soon, even our legs were caught in their tight embrace. I took a final stumbling step, then lost my balance completely, hitting the rough stone ground painfully. 'Ow!' I cried.

And so ends the quest, I thought sadly as I lay there all trussed up on the cold cobblestones. We would never get to the citadel now, never find the Ef-frock, never get a crimson cloak ...

'Going somewhere else already, so soon?' Squig asked.

Squig? Squig!

'You came for me!' I cried, almost moved to tears to see my quagga standing by my side. So quick was she that I had not even observed her arrival.

'Well, you called, didn't you?' she replied jovially, then picked me up in her mouth, rope and all, and tossed me on to her back.

'Wait, what about my friends?' I protested when Squig started moving off. The guards had already reached them and were forcing them to stand up. The hairy guard was now looking at me with a determined glint in his eye.

'No time!' Squig said merrily. Indeed, the hairy guard was now pointing the last remaining tree branch at Squig, and was beginning to yell, 'Release—'

But fortunately, his Krake-rope never reached my faithful quagga, for she had taken off at a run and was soon out of reach of the guard's magic.

'Help!' Mia screamed as I galloped away. My heart twisted inside me to see my two friends writhing in the clutches of the fearsome guards.

'Take heart!' I shouted back, frantically thinking of some uplifting words that could help comfort them in this hour of their darkest despair. 'Um … it could have been worse! Your insides could have turned into marshmallows!'

My last word echoed down the street: 'Mellows … mellows … mellows …' as Squig took me far, far away from both my enemies and my friends.

CHAPTER NINE

As I was all tied up, I could not hold on to Squig's mane and ended up bouncing along precariously, head hanging down one side of her back and legs down the other.

'Where to?' she asked after a while. She was running so fast that everything around me was a blur.

'Where are we?' I gasped. 'Where were you heading?'

'I'm just running round the city in circles. I've done three laps already.'

What should I do? Where should I go? We had formulated no plan, as we had thought we could rely on Karina to tell us what to do. Now that she had betrayed us and my sidekicks were captured, I felt more lost than ever.

'Just did two more!' Squig reported. 'Passing the citadel for the fifth time!'

The citadel! The Ef-frock was kept in the CATTSS' citadel. And surely that would be where the guards would bring the Overworld spies for questioning as well? To the citadel I should go then, to rescue my friends, steal the Ef-frock, and fulfil my destiny as a hero! Only, could I really do it on my own? To be honest, I did not have the faintest idea what I would do once I got to the citadel.

'Seven times! I'm on a roll!' Squig announced.

'Drop me off at the citadel the next time you pass it, will you?' I asked.

'Nope, I can't do that!' she replied cheerfully. 'Quaggas are not allowed to park anywhere near the city centre due to congestion control regulations. Any quagga found in violation will be painted and have to live out the rest of their lives in shame as a zebra.'

'Not even for a quick drop-off?'

'Not even that,' she confirmed.

'Where *can* you stop?'

Squig thought for a moment. 'I can let you get off at the river towards the northeast of the city. The river runs northeast–southwest, and the citadel sits atop the river right in the centre of the city. Follow the river and you won't miss it. It's the building with the tallest spire.'

As she spoke, she slowed down, and I saw we were now strolling on a promenade beside a beautiful river that sparkled under the glowing orb in the sky, which was their sun. Across the river, houses in all manner of splendour, many of them with short spires or turrets, lined the marina, while in the distance, I could see the city walls rising up protectively.

On our side of the river, the houses were smaller but nonetheless elegant, and many of them seemed to double as shops on the ground floor. The majority of the spires were congregated downriver, and in their midst was a particularly tall and imposing grey one topping a massive tower. Even from this distance, I could see that the sides of that spire were not smooth, but chased with countless intricate carvings.

'Thank you, Squig,' I said as I slid off her back. 'I won't forget your kindness.' I wanted to take her front hoof in my hand in friendship, then realized I was still all tied up. 'Um ... could you chew off this rope, by any chance?' I asked hopefully.

Squig recoiled in horror. 'Can you bite this railing by the river?' she asked in disgust, then disappeared in the puff of smoke caused by her lightning-quick departure.

I stared after her in shock, then sighed, hoping I had not damaged our relationship irredeemably with what Squig clearly saw as an insulting request. Fortunately, the rope ended at my calves and I was just able to move my feet, so I resigned myself to shuffling along the river like a duck as I headed southwest towards the citadel. Perhaps some of the pigeons hopping about nearby would take me for food and peck the rope off me.

No such luck.

Quaint, stone bridges spanned the river at regular intervals, and as I neared one of them, a stroke of inspiration struck me. Perhaps I could find a jagged stone edge on which I could cut the rope! I ambled over to the bridge, my gaze on the uneven surface of the stones, looking for a sharp point.

'Thank goodness, you're safe!' a familiar voice sounded behind me.

I whirled round to see Karina standing at the bottom of the steps that led from the promenade to the river's edge.

'You!' I exclaimed, lost my balance and rolled down the stairs, coming to a stop at her feet. Feeling rather dizzy from my fall, I lay there for a moment, gazing up into her face as she bent down to look at me. Silhouetted against the sun, her fine hair shimmering in the golden light, she seemed like an angel descended from heaven. Or *a devil ascended from hell*, I corrected myself, remembering her betrayal.

'I got to the city before you and thought I'd come in first,' she said. 'I was worried Tago would catch up with me if I loitered outside. When I was already in the city, I saw the Wanted poster at Mistress Malory's tavern. Good thing they haven't had time to paste them all over the city yet! I could only hope you'd evade the guards and make it to our meeting point.'

'You didn't tell me yonder where,' I complained.

'I said yonder bridge,' she said, looking surprised.

'Sure, it's the bridge over there, but over there where?'

'Here, of course!' She pointed to a bronze plate nailed to the base of the stairs. It read: 'Yonder Bridge'.

'This is Yonder Bridge?' I asked, still a little dazed.

'It sure is!' Karina replied.

I shook my head in astonishment. Who in the world would give a bridge such a confusing name? *Underworlders, apparently,* I thought ruefully.

Karina was cocking her head as she eyed me from head to toe. 'What happened to you? Why are you all tied up?'

I looked up into her eyes, so clear and bright with a child-like innocence. Was she telling the truth? After all, she had come here to meet me, just as she had promised. Could I really trust her again? I decided to test her with clever questions.

'Did you betray us?' I demanded.

'What? No!' she exclaimed.

'Wasn't it you who told the guards what we look like?'

'Of course not!'

'Are you sure?'

'Yes!'

'Okay,' I said, feeling vaguely disappointed that Karina had not revealed any information that would prove her guilt or innocence definitively.

'It must have been Tago,' she said, clenching and unclenching her fists in agitation. 'He knows you're with me, and he'll do it simply out of spite.'

I eyed Karina shrewdly. Tago could not have known we were Overworlders as we had already changed into our disguises when he arrived at Botuni's, our own clothes rolled up and hidden in our backpacks. Was Karina really the one who had betrayed us, like what Mia believed? I felt I could no longer trust her. However, if I continued to show my suspicion, she might turn me over to the city guards immediately. Besides, I needed help to understand the workings of this strange city. I decided to play along for now, then ditch her when I had got what I needed.

Karina was still seething, presumably thinking dark thoughts about Tago. 'Can you help me with this rope?' I asked.

Karina came out of her reverie with a start. Bending down, she tugged at the end of the rope, but that only served to make it tighten its coils even further, crushing the breath out of me as it did so.

Karina looked surprised. 'Oh, it's a Krake-rope. Why didn't you say so earlier?'

She took out from her backpack a small bottle with the label, 'Magical Influence Remover Emollient (MIRE)' and unscrewed the cap, which was attached to a dropper. She squeezed a few drops of blue liquid on the rope, and immediately, it unwound itself and turned back into a tree branch.

I recalled having seen the bottle of MIRE in Botuni's shop, but had resisted taking it because I didn't want to waste my backpack quota on something so small. Instead, I had taken a violin, complete with bow and case. I had been quite pleased with my decision at the time, as I figured that not only was the violin the biggest item I could find in the shop, but I had also wittily got round the six-item rule because technically, the violin, bow and case were three items but only counted as one. Now, however, I wondered if I had made a mistake. Probably not, but after all the missteps that had led to my friends' capture, I couldn't be entirely sure.

'Thanks,' I said, after sucking in a deep breath gratefully. Then, I added conversationally, 'That bottle looks really useful.'

'It is,' she said. 'MIRE works on all Level Six and below magic. I never go questing without it.'

I looked at it longingly, then sighed and scooped up the tree branch. 'I've lots to learn, haven't I?'

'Oh, you're not doing too badly,' Karina said warmly, and I felt the icicle in my heart melt a little.

I gave myself a mental shake. *The sweetest smile hides the most treacherous intentions*, I told myself firmly.

'What happened to Ryan and Mia?' Karina asked, holding out a hand to help me up.

'They were caught by the city guards,' I said, then recounted what had happened.

'Oh dear,' Karina commiserated. 'We must save them, of course. All the more we should head for the citadel. It's likely they'll be hauled there for questioning.'

That was exactly what I had thought, but now I wondered if she was leading me into a trap. Still, what choice did I have? I had no idea where else I could go.

Totally oblivious to my inner conflict, Karina said musingly as we began walking up the steps to get back to street level, 'The Ef-frock is hidden at the centre of a maze at the top of the citadel tower. The dungeons are located deep in the basements. We can sneak into the tower and try to get the Ef-frock first, then head down to the dungeons to rescue your friends.'

Clearly, she wanted to lead me into the citadel to be captured, but I planned to outsmart her when the time came. *I'll ditch her when I get to the maze,* I promised myself. *I know! I'll ditch her* in *the maze!*

I thought of the last object I had put into my backpack at Botuni's, not knowing then what I would use it for but astute enough to realize it was too useful to leave behind. It would be ideal for getting away from Karina and getting my revenge on her as well ... if I lived long enough to use it.

When we had climbed back up to the bridge, Karina pointed to the tallest spire with the carvings that I had noticed earlier. 'Yonder is the citadel.' Turning to the east, then north, west, and south, she pointed towards the distant city walls, 'And yonder are the entry and exit points from the city—there, there, there, and there. We entered from the eastern gate. After stealing the Ef-frock and rescuing your friends, we should follow the river for a distance, then veer left to escape by the southern gate because that is the nearest to the secret entrance to the Overworld.'

I nodded to show my compliance, but in my heart, I was resolving that once I had the Ef-frock, I would simply call my quagga and get a quick ride out of the city.

Karina continued, 'We have to escape on foot instead of calling our quaggas because quaggas can't park in the city centre, and they'll have trouble taking us through the city gates too.'

Drats.

'Can't we just harness the power of the Ef-frock to magic ourselves out?' I asked.

Karina looked like I had just punched her nose and then asked her for a reward. 'Of course not! Didn't I tell you that very few people know how to extract magic from the rock? Well, I'm not one of them, so just listen to me, okay? The way out is yonder.' And she pointed again to the southern gate, which

I could just make out as an arched gap in the long stretch of wall far away.

'Oh, *yonder*,' I said, the significance of the bridge's name dawning on me at last.

'That's right,' Karina said. 'This bridge is where you can get a good view of most of the important locations in the city.'

I stuck the tree branch into my belt like a sword, then we started for the citadel—the heart of the city and the seat of the CATTSS' power. As we walked, my thoughts turned to Mia and Ryan. They must be terribly frightened to have fallen into the clutches of the CATTSS' lackeys. What would happen to them? Would they be tortured? Would they be killed? And if I myself were caught, would the same thing happen to me? Would I ever get to see my parents again?

But I did not allow myself to dwell too long on such dark thoughts. For one thing, I was a little distracted by the sight of cute little ducklings swimming close to the banks of the river. For another, I knew I had to keep my spirits up, for I was my friends' only hope, and they were counting on me.

Part - II

CHAPTER TEN

'We can't count on our so-called leader,' Mia said as the cart she and Ryan were lying in trundled down the street. 'He's hopeless. We have to find a way to escape ourselves.'

Ryan lay beside her, his eyes squeezed tight, trying to stem his rising panic by taking deep breaths. Why did he have to come on this mission? *Breathe ...* Why did he let Mia bully him into doing something that was never in his nature in the first place? *Breathe ...* He could even now be sitting comfortably in bed, eating oatmeal while watching his favourite documentary. *Breathe ...*

The cart was being pulled by the unbelievably strong hairy guard. For the tenth time since Mia and Ryan became the unwilling passengers of this mode of transport, the cart rolled over a bump, jolting them painfully. They could not even brace themselves against the bone-rattling ride as they were still trussed up in the Krake-ropes.

'Books on fire! I swear he's doing this deliberately,' Mia muttered.

'I am!' the hairy guard called back jovially. 'No prizes for being right!'

'Where are they taking us?' Ryan whimpered, opening his eyes to take a peek, then shutting them again.

'I heard the guards say something about a fortress,' Mia replied.

Ryan gave a shudder. 'It's the citadel,' he said hoarsely. 'They're taking us to the CATTSS' citadel.'

'It's all his fault, if you think about it,' Mia said angrily.

'Who?' Ryan asked, confused.

'Who else? If he hadn't trusted Karina, we wouldn't have been betrayed. He should have listened when I tried to warn him.'

'Did you say you know Karina?' the hairless guard, who was walking next to the cart, remarked.

'So what if I did?' Mia retorted, not inclined to feel friendly towards one of the men who had captured her.

'A likely story,' the hairy guard sniffed. 'She's a councillor's daughter. As if she would hang out with Overworld scum like you!'

'I knew it!' Mia said triumphantly, snapping her head back to look at Ryan. 'She's one of them! She's a CATTSS spy!'

'Mia, can you please stop talking?' Ryan asked anxiously. He was afraid she would inadvertently give something away at this rate. So long as the CATTSS did not know what they were here for, they still had the chance to bluff their way out of their predicament.

But Mia was too worked up to keep quiet. 'I don't even see why he was chosen. The prophecy about him wasn't even real! I've put up with him, supporting him in every way I can, and what's he done? Nothing but mess things up and depend on his friends to make decisions and get him out of trouble.

And when the crisis hits, what does our dear leader do? He runs away, leaving us to the dogs!'

'Hey,' the hairy guard said. 'That's not very nice!'

'See?' Mia said to Ryan. 'Even the guards are offended by his behaviour. And instead of saying something useful when we separated, he talks some rot about marshmallows.'

Ryan murmured, 'Not marshmallows. He was quite faint but I managed to make out what he said: "Take all the plush pillows." I've been trying to figure out what he meant. I'm sure it must be something very important.' He thought of the number of times Julian had protected him from Mia's rage or sarcasm, and promised himself inwardly to devote all his mental faculties to decoding his esteemed friend and leader's message.

'That's ridiculous,' Mia scoffed. 'No, we can't depend on him any more,' she concluded with a toss of her chin. There was more that she could have said, things along the lines of herself being a better choice for a leader, and that perhaps Wuchiwark's discarded rhyme was about her, but she didn't want to appear too conceited. Oh, why had she persuaded Julian to take up the quest? She should have done it herself, with or without sidekicks. After all, she was the reincarnation of the great King Arthur. Perhaps it was a good thing they were separated from Julian. It would be the ideal chance for her to prove her worth.

Lost in her ruminations, she did not even realize they had reached their destination until the hairless guard said, 'Here we are!' The cart had slowed to a stop. Mia and Ryan twisted uncomfortably in their ropes to see where they were— an unnecessary gesture as the very next moment, the guards dragged them out of the cart into an upright position, where they then had a much better view with considerably less effort.

They were in a courtyard, standing before a great stone edifice designed like a large, medieval castle. Battlements ran along the parapets and narrow, elongated windows dotted the facade. From somewhere within this monstrous structure, a single tower rose up, stone upon stone upon stone, higher and higher until it peaked in a spire from which flew an enormous flag of the CATTSS—a light blue background adorned with a ferocious dragon. From the lack of pomp and decor in their surroundings, it was evident they were at the rear of the castle.

The hairless guard poured some sort of liquid on the ropes binding the kids, and immediately they unwound and sprang back into their original shapes. The guards then pushed the kids towards a small door, which was opened by a guard in red-and-gold livery. A short corridor led to the citadel's kitchen. Chaos seemed to be the order of the day, with three chefs running around frantically, taking care of pots that were bubbling over, kneading dough on a dirty countertop cluttered with containers and utensils, and chopping vegetables on boards that clearly needed a good scrub. The floor was littered with vegetable peel and spilt sauce.

'The CATTSS could learn a lesson or two from Mistress Malory about organizing a kitchen,' Mia remarked. 'It'll just take a couple of stickers.'

'Ah, you don't understand,' the hairless guard said, sighing. 'Since the CATTSS are the ones who issue the stickers, they can't be seen to abuse their power. They are afraid people will question the fairness in how the stickers are distributed. That's why all the citadel staff, whether working in the kitchen, toilets or chambers, are not allowed to use magic in their work. Only us guards,' he added, puffing his chest out proudly, 'may use it, since our job safeguards the realm, which benefits everyone.'

After passing the kitchen, they walked through several corridors separated by heavy stone archways, then went down a dark stairwell dimly lit by torches mounted on brackets at regular intervals on the circular wall, finally emerging into a spacious chamber where two doors broke the monotony of the stone bricks that made up the walls. A guard in the red-and-gold livery of the citadel was sitting at a table between the doors, eating peanuts. The entrance of a passageway could be seen at the other end of the chamber, but the darkness beyond it prevented the kids from seeing where it led.

Above the door to the left of the guard was the sign, 'Torture Chamber', and above the one on the right was written, 'Less Torturous Chamber'.

Please, let them put us in the room on the right, Ryan thought, quaking down to his boots. After exchanging greetings with the peanut guard, the hairy guard said, rubbing his palms in glee, 'Now the fun starts! I can't wait!'

'We'll start with me!' the hairless guard said, equally excited.

'No, no, no,' the hairy guard said. 'We always start with the bad cop.'

'But that's not fair!' protested the hairless guard. 'We should start with the good cop sometimes too!'

They're talking about the classic 'good cop–bad cop' routine, Ryan realized. Typically, the 'bad cop' would interrogate the prisoner, threatening them and hitting them, and just when things got really bad, the 'good cop' would take over, all nice and chummy, so the prisoner would be won over and spill the beans. And if that still didn't work, the 'bad cop' would be back, and so on, until the prisoner gave in to avoid falling into the brutal hands of the 'bad cop' again.

The hairy guard said, 'There's no point doing good cop first. They're not going to talk if you cosset them at the very beginning!'

'They might if I'm really nice!' the hairless guard said, beaming to show all his rotted teeth as a demonstration of how friendly he could be.

'Let's not waste time. You know how this works.'

'But you always end up killing them,' the hairless guard whined. 'Then I never get my share of fun.'

End up killing them? Ryan and Mia looked at each other, and being perfectly capable of reading simple expressions accurately, knew that both shared the same sense of alarm.

'I don't always kill them,' the hairy guard growled. 'I left one alive before, remember?'

'Only one,' the hairless guard grumbled. 'I only got to play good cop once, in all the twenty years we've worked together!'

'Better than nothing!' the hairy guard said cheerfully. 'Come, let's not waste any more time.'

And to the kids' horror, he proceeded to unlock the door named 'Torture Chamber' and shoved them in.

At first, they were blinded by a gaping darkness. Then, a light flared and a large brazier in the middle of the room came to life. It might have been better if it had not, for now Ryan and Mia could see that the room was filled with horrible implements of torture. A coffin-shaped box, with its door ajar on its hinges so the spikes on the inside of the door could be seen, stood in a corner. Racks displaying branding irons, finger-squashers, nail-pluckers, one-starred novels, and sheaves of poems that *did not rhyme* stood in another corner. Hanging from the ceiling were various ropes and chains, the uses of which the kids could not even begin to imagine.

After giving the kids enough time to inspect the torture instruments and get frightened, the guards pushed them into two chairs placed behind a small wooden table. The hairless guard then walked back to the door to stand with the peanut guard, who had ambled over, still cracking and chewing, to watch the show.

Then, the hairy guard stood menacingly over the kids from across the table, chuckling evilly.

'Now,' he said, 'will you tell me who you really are, and what you are doing in the Underworld?'

CHAPTER ELEVEN

The citadel was a mere two miles away, according to Karina. I don't think she understood what 'mere' really means, because by the time we were halfway there, my legs were already beginning to ache from the unaccustomed exercise. Thankfully, the weather was just nice—mild and with a touch of breeze.

Karina was in good spirits. She skipped along, pointing out various attractions to me as if she had forgotten we had a gruelling task at the end of our walk, which might well end in both our deaths. As I considered this sobering possibility, I could not help but think it surprising, even downright unbelievable, that a girl we had only just met would want to risk her life to help some people she barely knew. She must either have a very kind, selfless heart, or she was only pretending to help me and was actually a lackey of the CATTSS.

'Shh! A lackey of the CATTSS!' Karina suddenly said. I don't know why she shushed me since she had been the one talking, not me.

She pushed me behind a makeshift stall selling handcrafted jewellery. I waited a couple of seconds, then peeked out. A man with a great number of pockmarks on his face was walking with big, loping steps down the cobbled street in our direction. Every now and then, he would stop to ask a passer-by a question or peer behind stalls.

'Him?' I asked. 'But he's not in livery.'

'They don't always wear their uniform if they aren't on guard duty at the wall or at the citadel. But they always carry a Krake-rope. That's how I can tell.'

Indeed, the man had a tree branch clutched in his big fist.

'He's looking for you,' she whispered. 'We have to make a detour.' She glanced about, then pointed down an alleyway. 'Next time he turns around, we make a run for it.'

We watched him closely, and when he turned to talk to a fruit seller, we dashed across the street and into the alley.

'What if someone saw us come in here and gives us away?' I asked as we walked down the alley.

Karina looked at me admiringly. 'That's the smartest thing you've said all day.'

I blushed, unaccustomed to such praise. I was still fumbling for some clever response when she suddenly stopped walking and said excitedly, 'Look!'

I turned my gaze towards the door she was pointing at. A big signboard hung over it. 'The Soothy Sisters' Spectacular Stunt Show!' it proclaimed in a dramatic cursive font.

'The S-S-S-S-S?' I asked, trying to raise a quizzical eyebrow but only succeeding in moving my entire brow up and down.

'The Sssss,' Karina corrected me, pronouncing it like the hiss of a snake. 'I've always wanted to go, but Papa never had the time to bring me. Let's hide in there! The CATTSS lackey would never think to find us there, and I really do want to see the show!'

It was a difficult moment for me. On one hand, my two best friends had been captured, were very likely being tortured, and the only thing that stood between them and certain death was my timely arrival to save them. On the other hand, my current companion, whom I barely knew and who was almost certainly a CATTSS spy herself, wanted to fulfil her childhood dream of watching a stunt show while we were in the middle of a rather urgent quest on which the fate of an entire world rested. Did I really have time to stop?

Speaking of time, this reminded me of how much I hated timed examinations. Working within a time limit was totally not how my brain functioned. If I were given more time, say, an unlimited amount of it, no doubt I would be able to come up with all the right answers—

'What did you say?' Karina asked.

'Oh, er ...'

'Thank you!' she said, happily taking my non-committal answer for a 'yes'. The door yielded to her gentle push, and we walked into a large room, two-thirds of which was filled with spectators sitting on tiered wooden benches. A large stage decorated like an abandoned warehouse took up the rest of the space, and two muscular women were engaged in a mock fight while wielding flaming torches.

'There're some seats here,' Karina said, motioning me to follow her. We sat down at the front to the far left, where we had an off-centre but otherwise excellent view of the proceedings on stage.

The Soothy sisters were two women, probably in their thirties. One was tall and large-boned with a weather-beaten face while the other was a head shorter, smaller in build but extremely muscular, and had a no-nonsense look despite her gentler features.

Both Big and Small Soothy jumped and rolled and swung off various props on stage most agilely as they escaped each other's rehearsed attacks. Several times, the fire from the torches appeared to be on the verge of engulfing the performers, eliciting collective roars from the crowd. I had to admit then that, despite my earlier misgivings, I had made the right decision to pause in my quest to watch a stunt show. Being a hero was stressful business and taking time out to decompress was a perfectly legitimate use of time. Karina, for her part, could barely contain her delight. She crowed and gasped and clutched my arm as the sisters performed one amazing stunt after another.

Finally, they stopped their antics and stood beaming at the audience, receiving the thunderous applause as was their due.

'And now,' Big Soothy announced, 'comes the most popular part of our performance. Audience participation!'

The crowd cheered. Half the audience jumped up, waving their arms wildly.

'Me! Me!' Karina cried, pointing at herself with both thumbs.

'I choose you!' Big Soothy pointed to an old, shrunken gentleman from the other side of the room. He bounded up to the stage as if he were half his age, grinning inanely.

'And I choose you!' Small Soothy pulled from the audience a young woman. She gasped in delight and then fainted from the overwhelming emotion.

The Soothy sisters found a replacement for the young woman, then Big Soothy scanned the audience for their last volunteer. Almost the entire crowd had gone practically feral by this time, jumping up and down, waving frantically and hooting.

Looking at the frenetic behaviour around me, I couldn't help feeling amused. I never did get this thing about audience participation. I mean, people paid good money (I hadn't paid any yet for this show, come to think of it) to watch an act performed by professionals, so why would they want to watch some unqualified audience member bumming about on stage? Where was the fun in that?

At that moment, Big Soothy's gaze was sweeping across the room in our direction. Karina's arms were windmilling about wildly.

Big Soothy finally made her selection. 'And … it will be … you!'

She was pointing right at me. But why? I had not raised my hand!

'Go, go!' Karina urged, evidently wishing to enjoy the experience by proxy.

I stood up hesitantly, but did not want to draw attention to myself by refusing, so I went up to the stage where three hundred pairs of eyes focused on me, watching my every move.

Big Soothy said, 'It's very simple. Just follow my instructions and no harm will come to you. Now, you, Mister,' speaking to the old gentleman, 'when I blow my whistle, you must stand very still.'

The old man nodded eagerly. The other volunteer and I moved aside to give the sisters space to do their stunt. Big Soothy held a large hoop ringed with fire to one side of the short gentleman, on a level with his head, while Small Soothy leapt over him and through the hoop without singeing herself. Claps erupted all over the room and the old man went back to his seat with an exhilarated look that said his life would never be the same again.

'And you, Miss,' Big Soothy said, 'when I blow my whistle, you must raise your arm like this.'

The young woman did as told, and Small Soothy wheeled under her arm on a flaming unicycle, to general applause. The young woman skipped back to her seat happily.

I was beginning to look forward to my turn. How exciting to be part of a wonderful act like this, even if it wasn't much fun for the audience!

'And you, little lad,' Big Soothy said, whereupon I stepped up eagerly, 'when I blow my whistle, you must spin around, run to this two-storey ladder, climb to the top, crawl through that barrel, leap across those crates, climb down the rope, take four medium-sized steps forward, crouch down, do a somersault, then eat five turkey legs within a minute. Don't deviate from the instructions even one bit as balls of fire will be raining down from our contraption up there. If you're not where you're supposed to be at the time, you'll be burnt alive!'

I gulped. 'Actually, I'm not—' I began to protest, but Big Soothy had put the whistle to her lips. 'CATTSS lackey,' she hissed just loud enough for me to hear, her voice dripping with venom, then the whistle went off, and I turned and fled for the ladder as fireballs began falling behind me.

CHAPTER TWELVE

Ryan and Mia shrank against their seats as the hairy guard sat on the table and leant closer towards them.

'So, why did you come to the Underworld?' he snarled.

'We ... we're tourists,' Mia said stoutly.

'Nonsense!' he shouted, slamming his burly fist down on the table. 'The guardian swans have told us how your army of six hundred soldiers overwhelmed them after three days and three nights of battle. Does that sound like something tourists would do?'

The swans lied to cover up their own mistake, Ryan thought. *Spineless creatures!*

'We have no army,' he whimpered. 'We're just kids!'

'Don't think you can fool me! Those—' the hairy guard gestured to our backpacks, which the hairless guard was holding, 'are standard-issue adventurer's backpacks. You are clearly on a quest. Confess! What is it you are after?'

'We really are tourists,' Mia said plaintively. 'We just like being prepared in a foreign country.'

The hairy guard's face had been slowly turning red and now he jumped up in a fury. 'I can't stand it any longer!' he yelled, then stomped towards the rack of torture implements. Ryan and Mia cowered closer to each other, watching fearfully to see which tool he would pick up.

Not the poems! Don't let it be the poems, Ryan prayed feverishly.

The guard came back with a long cane that had five curved prongs at one end.

He's going to peel off our fingernails, one prong for each nail! Ryan thought fearfully.

He's going to stick that down our throats and claw out our entrails! Mia thought with horror.

The hairy guard proceeded to use the back scratcher to claw his back while saying apologetically to his fellow guards, 'Sorry … been fighting this itch for a long time.'

Ryan and Mia exchanged relieved glances.

After a while, the hairy guard put down the stick and glowered at the prisoners. 'Now, where was I? Oh yes, you were about to confess why you are here. Say it!' he bellowed. 'Say it! Don't make me have to force you!'

A whimper escaped Ryan's lips. The man was so loud! Did he have to be so loud? Ryan could feel his insides dissolving. He felt that any longer of this and he would confess to anything.

After a moment of silence, the hairy guard roared, 'So you do want me to force you! Don't blame me then!' He bent down such that the kids' view of him was momentarily blocked by the table.

What is he up to? Mia wondered, trying not to let her panic show. Were there torture instruments under the table too? She hadn't noticed. The other guards were retreating rapidly from the door of the chamber, looks of consternation on their faces. Was the hairy guard going to throw an explosive at them or something?

After a few intense seconds, the kids became aware of a horrible stench. It smelt like rotten eggs and rancid meat sprinkled with a dash of sewer waste, and it was getting stronger and stronger ...

The hairy guard had been taking off his boots and now he sat down on the table and swung his stockinged feet over towards the kids.

Death by smelly socks! Ryan realized, shocked at how ruthless the guard was to use this ancient form of torture on them. *We're doomed*, he thought, as he and Mia recoiled in horror. Across the doorway, the hairless guard and the peanut guard were both holding their noses and trying not to retch.

'Now you will tell me,' the hairy guard said, smiling craftily, 'are you spies from the Overworld?'

Ryan and Mia shook their heads mutely, trying hard not to breathe.

'Did you overpower the guardian swans?'

Again, they shook their heads, their faces puffing up from the exertion of holding their breaths.

'Were you the ones who made a hole in the grate leading from the citadel's cellar to the river, making it look like rust damage?'

'Freaking round tables!' Mia could not help exclaiming at the ridiculousness of the guard's questions and directly received a powerful whiff of his malodorous foot coverings. Bile rose up in her throat but she forced it down through the sheer force of her will. No way was she going to disgrace herself in front of this detestable guard!

Undeterred by Mia's scorn, their interrogator continued firing off a series of questions: 'Did you poison the citadel guards so that most of them are now ill with diarrhoea, with only four left to guard the entire citadel? Did you attempt to climb up the citadel tower to steal the Ef-frock located within the maze at its peak? Are you trying to overthrow the CATTSS? Did you steal my nail-clipper?'

Ryan felt that he could not hold out much longer. He had to either take a breath or die of suffocation. Deciding that the latter was preferable, he clamped his fingers more tightly around his nose, but his strength was waning. Already, his vision was dimming ...

'That's enough now,' someone called from outside the room. It was the hairless guard. 'You promised you'll let me have my turn of fun and our shift is almost over.'

Grumbling beneath his breath, the hairy guard pulled on his boots. Ryan let himself take in a breath and clutched the edge of the table for support. The smell was still there, though not half as bad as before; he could just about bear it. Mia looked rather green in the face from her earlier ordeal, but her relief was plain to see as well.

The hairless guard came in to escort them out of the room. As they got to their feet weakly, both were assailed by the same desperate thought: they had survived the first round of torture, but would they survive the next?

I must work out what Julian meant when he said 'take all the plush pillows' before it's too late, Ryan thought feverishly. He was certain that Julian had spoken in such an enigmatic code because he trusted Ryan would be able to break it, and he was determined not to let his best friend down.

I must escape from this place and whack Julian over the head for getting us into this mess, Mia was thinking. And then she almost cried at the thought that by the time their interrogators were done with them, she might never see him, or any of her friends and family, again.

CHAPTER THIRTEEN

The fireballs started dropping the moment the whistle went off.

What were Big Soothy's instructions? Fear for my life gave my mind instant clarity: climb ladder, crawl through barrel, leap over crates, climb down rope, take four medium steps, somersault, eat turkey legs. I salivated at that last thought and, wiping a hand across my drooling mouth, moved as quickly as I could.

I only barely managed to keep one step ahead of the danger. Reaching the ladder, I leapt on to the first rung and immediately discovered to my dismay that it was very loosely secured to the upper deck of the warehouse set. It wobbled ominously as I sprang up the steps, and collapsed entirely the moment I had one foot on the upper floor. As the ladder fell away below me, I pushed myself forward with a desperate yelp to avoid plummeting to the ground and ended up sprawled face down on the dusty deck.

Phew! Tragedy averted. I turned my head to give Karina a victorious smile, but she was gesticulating frantically at a point above me. I looked up to see a gigantic ball of flame hurtling down and rolled aside just before it crashed down beside me. Fortunately, the floorboards did not catch fire; they must have been covered with some flame-retardant coating to protect the performers. Lucky me!

I lay there panting while thinking furiously—an exercise that my brain was not accustomed to and hence took quite a bit of concentration. Big Soothy had called me a 'CATTSS lackey'. Why would she think I worked for the CATTSS? It wasn't as if I was walking around carrying a big Krake-rope … *Jousting knights!* I thought, falling back on Mia's method of cursing in my moment of shock. I *was* carrying a Krake-rope!

Karina's voice pierced through the fog of my mind: 'Look out!'

I snapped out of my reverie to see another fireball heading right for me. I rolled again and narrowly missed the fireball. I could feel the heat against my skin as it shattered beside me, leaving glowing bits of embers all around that still radiated intense heat. I was now pressed against the wall. There was nowhere else for me to roll if another fireball came down.

I scrambled to my feet and saw the open mouth of a wooden barrel staring at me. Oh yes, I was supposed to crawl through a barrel! Thankfully, it was huge—probably meant for someone the size of Big Soothy—so I had no difficulty fitting into it. Come to think of it, this whole stunt was almost definitely meant for the Soothies to perform, not a volunteer! Why did they hate the CATTSS so much that they would attempt to stage an accident with one of their lackeys? Would I survive long enough to find out? If only I had some magic to help me. Too bad our last sticker was with Ryan!

At that thought, I realized that I was still carrying my standard-issue adventurer's backpack. It was so small and light that I barely noticed its weight. Perhaps there was something in there that would be of some use. Now, what had I taken from Botuni's shop? By this time, I was feeling so panicked that my mind was a blank and I simply couldn't remember. I shrugged off the backpack frantically and started digging in it. Shielded as I was from the audience by the barrel, nobody could see what I was doing, which bought me some time.

Feeling around in the bag, my fingers closed around the neck of the violin case. Probably not very useful to start playing a ditty while fireballs were raining on my head, I decided, although I had just thought of a song that would go very well with what was happening.

I let go of the violin case reluctantly and searched around again, whereupon my fingers came into contact with a jar of 'Auntie Milly's Homemade Cookies' and the secret weapon I planned to use against Karina later. Again, neither of these items would be useful for this situation. Then there were a couple of erasable pens that I thought was pure genius and magic combined, which I put aside regrettably as unsuitable to the purpose of saving my life. (Ryan told me later we had such pens in our world too. To think I had been struggling with correction tape all this while!) Finally, I came upon my rolled-up bundle of Overworlder's clothes, which I concluded was not useful either, but ... what was this whitish stain on my jeans? *Oh, bird poo! Yucks!* With that thought, I suddenly remembered the poo-stained sticker I had put into my jeans pocket. What Level was it?

The Soothy sisters were getting impatient. They shouted, 'Get out of that barrel, you coward!' and other such encouragements. They even helpfully began to rain fireballs over my barrel. I could hear the thumps and feel the flares of heat as they impacted the surface of my cover. I knew that even with fire-retardant coatings, the barrel could well break down under the repeated barrage.

I thrust a hand into my jeans pocket and pulled out the sticker. A Level Nine! What luck! Praying that it was powerful enough for my purpose, I peeled off the backing and pasted the sticker on my chest, under my shirt. Putting a finger on it, I whispered, 'Protect me from fireballs!'

At that moment, I felt a heavy whack to the barrel and it burst into flames! I cowered against the heat, but amazingly, felt only a cool breeze wafting across my face.

The barrel split open as the fire ate at the wood, and like a phoenix rising from its fiery ashes, I stood up slowly amid the crackling flames, a brilliant smile on my lips.

The audience erupted with uproarious cheers, maniacal hand clapping, and thunderous feet thumping.

'More, more, more!' they chanted.

They wanted more heroic stuff? Sure! I walked leisurely across the floor towards some crates while casually flicking fireballs off my shoulders. Instead of leaping across the crates as instructed, I crawled over—somewhat inelegantly I must admit, but I was afraid of heights and standing up tall on creaky crates on the second floor of a makeshift warehouse set was not my idea of fun.

I climbed down the rope at the end of the crates to reach the floor of the stage, took four steps forward as instructed, got hit by a fireball in the head, realized my steps must be smaller than the Soothy sisters', and took another step forward. I then did a somersault and ended up in front of a low table where five delicious-looking roasted turkey legs were laid out on a platter.

The crowd went wild. They had evidently never seen anyone finish off five turkey legs in under a minute. I was barely done wiping off the grease from my lips when they surged up to me, clamouring for my autograph. Unfortunately, I didn't have a pen (or rather, I had two, but they were in my backpack that I'd left on the upper floor of the warehouse set) and anyway, Big Soothy announced, 'Thank you, the show is over! Please put your tips in the jar at the door!' Muscular bouncers appeared from the shadowy corners of the room and herded the crowd towards the exit. Soon, I found myself alone in the room with the two Soothy sisters and Karina.

'You did it!' Karina gushed and threw herself into my arms. I returned her embrace awkwardly, hoping my face was not as red as it felt.

Big Soothy cleared her throat—a deep, rumbling sound that put me in mind of an imminently erupting volcano. I backed away warily, dragging Karina with me. 'I can explain about the Krake-rope—' I began.

Big Soothy cut me off. 'I must apologize.'

What? Was this a feint, intended to catch me out?

Small Soothy was holding up my backpack, my slightly singed clothes still spilling out from it. 'We didn't realize you were an undercover Overworlder until we saw your clothes,' she said. 'Forgive us for our impulsiveness earlier, though of course our little tricks could never faze someone of your heroic status!'

I tightened the cross-strings at the front of my shirt self-consciously, hoping the sticker was not visible through it. 'Um,' I mumbled.

'What better way to go undetected than to pretend to be a CATTSS lackey!' Big Soothy marvelled, pointing at the Krake-rope tucked into my belt.

'Uh, yes, that was my intent,' I agreed.

'But why do you hate the CATTSS so much?' Karina asked.

'Ah,' Big Soothy said sadly, 'not many people remember this, but our troupe used to be called The Soothy Sisters' and Brothers' Spectacular Stunt Show!'

'Ss-brr-sss?' Karina tried out the abbreviation. It sounded like the death gurgles of a strangled lizard.

'Exactly,' Big Soothy replied. 'A CATTSS councillor said our name would sound better without the "brothers", so our two brothers were arrested and tortured to death.'

'They did that just because they didn't like your name?' I asked, aghast.

The Soothies exchanged glances. Small Soothy gave a barely perceptible nod, and Big Soothy said, 'We think we can be honest with you. The truth is, shortly before their arrest, our brothers went into the citadel to perform for the councillors. They never came back. Next thing we knew, their dead bodies were carted out of the citadel, stinking of smelly socks. My sister and I suspect they saw or heard something they were not supposed to when they went into the citadel. Our troupe's name was just an excuse for the CATTSS to silence them.'

'What wickedness!' I exclaimed, expecting Karina to chime in as well. When she remained silent, I looked at her and noticed that she seemed troubled.

Before I could think further about Karina's reaction, Small Soothy asked, 'Is the prophecy finally coming true, after all these years? Is that why you're here?'

I had forgotten how well-known the prophecy was in the Underworld. 'Yes,' I admitted.

'"This boy will find the hidden key, in the form of a glowing rock,"' Big Soothy recited. 'That's the Ef-frock, isn't it?'

Again, I nodded. No point denying the obvious.

'How do you propose to get it?' she asked. 'Nobody knows where it's hidden except the CATTSS' lackeys.'

I glanced at Karina. She had told me the Ef-frock was in a maze at the top of the citadel tower, but had conveniently neglected to mention that only CATTSS' lackeys knew that. In the face of my silent accusation, her face hardened but she remained obstinately silent. I would have to find a chance to confront her, but now was not the time. If the Soothy sisters found out she was a CATTSS spy, that would be the end of her.

'I heard it's hidden at the top of the citadel tower,' I said neutrally.

'How resourceful of you!' Small Soothy said admiringly. 'If anyone is going to overthrow the CATTSS, it will be you!'

'Overthrow the CATTSS?' I repeated in alarm. 'That wasn't—'

'We'll help you get the Ef-frock!' Big Soothy interrupted. 'Any enemy of the CATTSS is a friend of ours. With our acrobatic prowess, we'll help you to get up the tower.'

'I was thinking of just climbing the stairs,' I confessed.

'No way!' Small Soothy exclaimed. 'The citadel is guarded by a hundred armed guards. If there were just, say, three or four guards, you could perhaps still manage to sneak in or overpower them, but with a hundred, it's impossible! You must instead scale the sheer, 200-metre tall tower from the outside.'

I forced a shaky smile and said weakly, 'Luckily I have you to help me then.'

'Give us a few minutes. We'll pack a few essentials, then we can be on our way.'

I nodded, relieved at the chance to get a few minutes' rest. My gymnastics on stage had tired me out and I sank into a front-row seat gratefully. Karina sat down beside me while the two Soothies bustled about backstage. This would be a good time to question Karina. Once we restarted our journey to the citadel, we would not have any time alone.

How should I broach the subject? Should I be gentle and subtle, intimating with roundabout hints that I knew she was not who she seemed, or take a more brusque and direct approach? What should I do if she started crying? Should I show sympathy or remain impartial? If she said she was hungry, should I let her have a snack? *Decisions, decisions, decisions,* I thought drowsily. *I'll make them later. Just need … a short … nap …*

I closed my eyes and promptly fell asleep.

CHAPTER FOURTEEN

The hairless guard ushered Ryan and Mia into the room labelled 'Less Torturous Chamber'. Unlike the room they had just vacated, this one was lit by aromatic candles placed in corners of the room. The fragrance from the candles and their gently flickering light gave the room a warm, cosy feel. Paintings depicting calm, pastoral scenes hung on cool, lilac walls. A soft, plush carpet lined the floor and several comfortable-looking armchairs stood around a coffee table decorated with origami cranes and a dainty tea set.

'Sit down, sit down,' the hairless guard urged. 'Would you like some tea?' He hovered over them, eager to please.

'Uh, sure?' Mia said.

After they were all settled comfortably and drinking a pleasant, refreshing brew that tasted of fresh flowers plucked with the first dew of the morning, the hairless guard leant forward with a confiding air and said, 'You know, there's no point refusing—'

'Shift's over!' the hairy guard shouted from outside.

'Oh, man!' the hairless guard complained, one hand rubbing his bald pate ruefully. 'I've only just started. It's always like this. I *never* get to have my share of fun.'

'You can continue the fun tomorrow,' Ryan said hopefully.

'No, I won't,' the guard said bitterly. 'My partner will insist on starting the day with the torture. He says mornings are the best times for squeezing information out of criminals. "Whack them before they're fully awake," is what he says. And after that, you'll be dead. Poor me.'

Ryan's eyes widened in alarm. He thought he might faint.

'What will happen to us tonight?' Mia asked, unable to hide the quiver in her voice.

The hairy guard did not seem pleased that both prisoners showed no sympathy whatsoever for his situation. 'You'll be locked up in the dungeon cell. My partner will come get you tomorrow morning,' he replied curtly.

'You could continue interrogating us tonight. All night, even,' Ryan said desperately, not liking the sound of 'dungeon cell'. His mind conjured up visions of dark, dank stone prisons infested with rats.

The hairy guard shook his head. 'We don't work overtime in the Underworld because life is good here. Come, follow me.'

The two kids put down their cups reluctantly and returned to the outer chamber with the guard. He led them down the dark passage at the other end, lighting the way with a bright torch. The peanut guard brought up the rear.

At the end of the passage was a great iron door, which the peanut guard unlocked with a massive iron key. The door creaked open and the kids were shoved inside.

'Wait!' Mia said, but the door banged shut behind them and they could hear the key turn in the lock. They were trapped.

***

Ryan looked at Mia fearfully. 'What should we do?'

'You might want to have a hot bath, or a nap,' suggested a voice from deep within the cell.

Except that it did not look anything like a cell.

It looked like a five-star hotel.

Heavy drapes of a deep, rich crimson hung across the wide walls, giving the impression of hiding large windows behind them. The peach-coloured carpet was even deeper and softer than that of the 'Less Torturous Chamber'. A low tea table and several cushions took up a small corner of the room in front of a cosy fireplace while four king-sized beds were lined against the walls, each adorned with four fluffy pillows and a beautiful quilt. And on the bed nearest to the door sat a curious-looking old man.

He was short and rather plump. A neatly trimmed white beard complemented the thick, white eyebrows and long, silky silver hair that hung down to his waist.

'Who are you?' Mia asked when she had finished gaping at her surroundings in astonishment.

'A prisoner, just like you,' he replied, then hopped down from the bed and walked over to them.

'Are all their dungeons like this?' Mia asked, sweeping her hand to indicate the magnificence surrounding them.

'Oh, there are only a few, and then hardly any prisoners. There isn't a lot of crime here, you know, and when there is, Hairy almost always tortures them to death, so there's no one left to lock up. But surely you know this; everyone knows this …' The old man paused, looking at them askance. 'But you don't … which means you're not from around here … you're Overworlders!'

He gazed at them, his face filled with wonder. 'Is the prophecy about to be fulfilled at last?'

'We don't know anything about any prophecy,' Mia said warily. Who knew if this old man was a CATTSS spy, planted here to dig out information from them unawares?

'You don't trust me,' the old man said shrewdly. 'And well that you shouldn't. Miaowi is cunning, to say the least. We haven't had a person like that in the Underworld in over a thousand years. It's good that you're cautious. It bodes well for your quest.'

Ryan had been staring at the old man with his brow creased, and now he brightened up. 'I was wondering why you look so familiar. You look like someone we know, only, better groomed, and a little … er …' He paused, embarrassed to have nearly committed a faux pas.

'Fatter?' the old man finished for him.

'Oh no, you're not fat,' Ryan said, eager to make up for his earlier mistake. 'You're just … er … stout.'

But the old man did not seem offended at all. In fact, he seemed excited by Ryan's words, his eyes twinkling from behind folds of stoutness.

Mia gave a start as she, too, saw what Ryan had already noticed. 'Rusty swords! You … you're …'

'I'm Wuchichoc,' he said, nodding. 'I see you have already met my brother, Wuchiwark.'

The resemblance was uncanny. There could be no doubt as to this old man's identity.

'Why are you in this five-star—I mean, dungeon?' Mia asked.

Wuchichoc sighed. 'Sit down. It's a long story. Tea?'

For the second time in half an hour, the kids were treated to a delicious concoction, this time tasting of autumnal blossoms steeped in snow melted from the highest alps. There was also a tray filled with delectable treats, ranging from biscuits to buns to candy.

'Wark and I were both CATTSS councillors,' Wuchichoc began, after the kids had each helped themselves to a biscuit. 'About fifteen years ago, a young man named Miaowi rose to the position as well, taking over from one who had just retired. He was a very hard worker. In fact, nobody had ever seen the likes of him. When everyone was resting, he would be poring over council documents, trying to make improvements everywhere. He was so enthusiastic about the work that within two years, almost without our realizing it, he had taken over our duties in many areas of importance—the staffing of the citadel, the issuance of magic stickers, the regulations on inter-world travel, the selection of cookies for the pantry … And why not? He was so efficient and effective, and so *happy* to be doing it.'

'I'll bet you were happy too,' Mia muttered.

'We were,' Wuchichoc admitted. 'We had more time for the higher pursuits of life—dragon-taming, quagga-riding … oh yes, it was a happy time.'

'Then what went wrong?' Ryan asked.

'Some of the reforms that he implemented were too heavy-handed. For example, he was worried that people would think we were abusing our power by using magic for our own benefit. So, he banned the use of stickers within the citadel.'

'We heard about that,' Ryan said.

'It was a difficult time. The citadel staff were not used to doing everything by hand.'

'They still aren't, from the looks of it,' Mia said, thinking of the messy kitchen they had passed by earlier.

'Ah, but it was worse in the beginning. And the impact of the reform was far-reaching. In fact, Wark's wife was one of the victims.'

'What?' Ryan and Mia exclaimed in unison.

Wuchichoc nodded gravely. 'There was a reception held at the citadel, and all the councillors' spouses were invited to attend. It was a fairly routine function; nothing out of the ordinary. But the cleanliness of the kitchen, without the help of magic, was appalling. The result was mass food poisoning. Miaowi refused to allow the use of stickers within the citadel, so everyone who attended the reception had to let the illness take its course. Most were ill for two to three days. Wark's wife, however, wasn't so lucky.'

'She was ill for four or five days?' Mia asked, tongue in cheek, but Wuchichoc's reply made her wish she had bitten it instead.

'She was dead in four or five days.'

CHAPTER FIFTEEN

'Too bad you don't have any stickers,' Big Soothy remarked. 'Teleporting up there will be so much easier.'

'You think?' Karina said wistfully.

We both gazed up at the ridiculously tall spire, the gigantic flag with its dragon emblem seeming like a small handkerchief from the ground.

The Soothy sisters put down the large, woven baskets they had been carrying on their shoulders and busied themselves tying them together, then attaching some ropes to them, while Karina and I looked around us. Even though this was the rear of the citadel, we had thought it would have been better guarded than this. In fact, there was no one around at all.

'Do you think we should take the stairs after all?' I asked, not quite looking forward to the promised outdoor experience. 'There doesn't seem to be many guards.'

'That's because they're all inside,' Small Soothy said while taking off her shoes. 'Okay, we're ready! You two get into the baskets. Big and I will climb up the tower using our bare hands and feet while balancing the baskets between us.'

'Is it dangerous?' I asked, testing the sturdiness of the baskets with my fingers nervously.

'Of course it is!' Big Soothy said, looking a little offended at my insinuation that it might not be. 'Any stunt that is worth doing is always dangerous.'

With that assurance, Karina and I climbed in gingerly. The sisters tied the ends of the ropes around their torsos, then hefted the baskets purely with the strength of their formidable core muscles, for their hands were already feeling along the stone wall for cracks that they could curl their fingers and toes into. Then, they started to climb, our two baskets bumping against each other with the movement.

It was the most terrifying experience of my life.

'This is the most terrifying experience of my life!' Small Soothy said happily as we began to ascend.

'Me too!' Big Soothy replied equally gaily.

At least some of us are enjoying this, I thought, trying to cheer myself up as well.

As the Soothy sisters slowly pulled themselves upwards using various footholds and handholds that were invisible to my eyes, the baskets were dragged along, and they shuddered horribly against the wall. I trembled with each vibration in my skin and was constantly bracing myself for the sudden drop that would come if either one of the sisters lost her grip. I knew Karina was also frightened, for she clutched the edge of her basket so tightly that her knuckles were all white.

But the sisters were nothing if not skilled, and so perfectly coordinated with each other that despite Big Soothy being a head taller than her sister, they climbed at exactly the same speed so the baskets were kept level. At no time did Karina or I feel like we were going to topple out.

Just as I was beginning to relax, we rose high enough for the winds that swirled among the many spires of the city to begin buffeting us, making the baskets sway—ever so slightly at first, then more vigorously the higher we climbed. I could see that the Soothies were finding the going tougher as well. Their grins had given way to grimaces as the winds whipped their hair and clothing relentlessly.

My heart was pounding in my chest and my mouth suddenly felt very dry. One mistake by a sister or a sudden gust of wind, and we could all fall to our deaths. The poor Soothy sisters would never get their revenge, I would never get to save the world nor my friends, and Karina ... well, I had no idea what Karina wanted. I looked at her, sitting so pale and quiet in her basket. Who was she really? Why was she risking her life to help me in this quest? If I died now, I would never know. This was as good a time as any to question her, I decided. In fact, this was my last chance.

'Karina ...' I began.

She turned her face towards me expectantly, but before I could continue, Big Soothy announced, 'Here we are!'

Looking up, I realized that while I was in my reverie, we had arrived just below an open window at the top of the tower.

Karina clambered out of her basket and on to the ledge of the window, balancing precariously for a second before hopping off into the tower. I followed her, then turned back to face the Soothies.

What could I say to two people who had just risked their lives to help me? What thanks could be sufficient for such a sacrifice? What words to convey the immense debt owed?

'Bird poo!' I told them.

The Soothy sisters adroitly flattened themselves against the wall while clinging on to the window ledge and successfully avoided being hit by the droppings of a pigeon that was flying over them.

'Thanks!' Small Soothy said. 'We owe you one.'

'Consider it even,' I said generously.

'Take care, hero from the legends,' Big Soothy said, hanging on to the wall with only one hand while using the other to remove some stray strands of hair from her face.

'It's our honour to have been a small part of your journey. Perhaps we will be remembered in the songs they will sing of you for generations after,' Small Soothy added, removing both hands to adjust her clothing while supporting herself against the wall with only her feet.

From that, I guessed they would have no difficulty getting off the tower now that Karina and I were no longer dead weights they had to manage.

And so I was stupefied when the sisters simultaneously pushed off the tower and started plummeting towards the distant ground, their baskets trailing behind them. I gasped, looking around for any eagles that might suddenly swoop under the falling Soothies to save them. Seeing none, I gasped again and covered one eye to halve the horror of what was to come.

However, when they were about halfway down, some cloth that had been hidden among the weaves of the baskets billowed out, and the sisters parachuted safely to the ground.

I turned around and slid down on to my buttocks, weak with relief. Karina dropped down beside me, and together we surveyed the scene before us.

We were seated at a junction, where stone corridors led off to the front and right. There were sconces on the walls, which illuminated the maze well enough for us to see that the passages did not run straight but turned gradually, such that we could not see beyond a few metres.

'So, we're finally here,' Karina said.

'Yes, we're finally here,' I echoed ominously, thinking of the special object in my backpack that I had been saving for this moment. Should I use it on Karina? There would be no turning back once I did.

'I never imagined,' she said softly, 'when I started out on my walk today, that my life would be so utterly changed.'

'Is it a good change?' I asked, glad for an excuse to delay executing my plan, although her comment came as a surprise to me.

'It could be,' she said, turning her face towards me. She was smiling, but her eyes were sad. Why?

Her voice was a little shaky when she continued, 'Whatever happens next, I want you to know that I never meant you any harm. Your friendship is the best thing that has happened to me in a long time, and I will always treasure the memory of our day together.'

Exactly what I wanted to say to her before severing our ties completely! What were the odds?

'I feel the same way too,' I told her awkwardly, and to cover up my embarrassment, I busied myself with my backpack and pulled out the special item. It broke my heart to use such a thing on her, but I told myself firmly that it was for the greater good of the entire Overworld. Once she used the item, she would no longer be able to see me, and I could sneak off into the maze alone, thus throwing her off my scent finally. I would miss her terribly, but now that I was so close to the object of my quest, I could not afford to let a CATTSS spy foil my plans at the last minute.

'It's been a long, tiring day,' I said. 'Won't it be a good idea to take a little rest before we enter the maze?'

She stared at the green eye mask that I held in my hand—the kind that airlines sometimes gave out on long-haul flights to help passengers sleep. With astonishment in her eyes, she too dug into her backpack and brought out an identical mask, except that it was grey.

'I took one from Botuni's shop for you too!' she exclaimed. 'I thought you would need some good sleep since you're on a stressful quest.'

I was touched beyond words that she was so concerned for my well-being. I wished she had thought to give it to me while I dozed at the Soothy sisters' arena though. The lights there had been particularly bright and my nap had not been as restful as it could have been. Still, better late than never, and I accepted the gift gratefully.

'Let's take a ten-minute power nap,' Karina suggested.

We swapped eye masks with a solemnity that made the action seem oddly ritualistic. I could not help feeling as if we were exchanging gifts in a pledge of something significant, though I could not figure out what.

'On a count of three,' Karina said softly.

I nodded.

'One …'

We lifted our eye masks.

'Two …'

We faced each other, our eyes meeting.

'Three …'

Darkness.

'No talking.' Karina's tremulous voice sounded very close to my ears.

'No talking,' I agreed, thinking it would be easier for me to sneak off that way.

I counted silently to 200. About three minutes of our ten-minute power nap was over. It should be safe for me to make a move now and get far enough away so Karina could not catch up with me when she took off her eye mask at the end of the stipulated period.

I slipped the eye mask over my head and blinked to get used to the light again.

Only then did I realize that Karina was gone. She had given me the slip, and I was now all alone in the maze.

CHAPTER SIXTEEN

'Wuchiwark's wife died of the food poisoning?' Mia said in dismay, ashamed of her earlier cheekiness.

Ryan ran a hand over his eyes. 'Poor Wuchiwark,' he whispered.

Wuchichoc sighed. 'His wife had just given birth, you see, so she wasn't as strong as she should have been. When she died, their daughter Karina was just a few weeks old—'

'Who did you say?' Mia interrupted.

'Wark's wife …'

'No, I mean the daughter,' Mia said impatiently.

'Karina?'

'Their daughter's name is Karina?' Ryan asked, his eyes wide. He remembered one of the guards mentioning that Karina was a councillor's daughter, but he had not made the connection then. Why didn't Karina tell them she was Wuchiwark's daughter? She knew they were on a mission from him. Why the secrecy?

'You know her?' Wuchichoc asked.

'We met her earlier today,' Mia explained. 'She said she was going to help us with our quest. Then, when we got to the city, she disappeared and guards came chasing after us. We think she betrayed us.'

'Do you think she would?' Ryan asked Wuchichoc, anxious to give Karina the benefit of the doubt.

Wuchichoc looked solemn. 'I don't know her well enough to judge her. She was a mere baby when I was thrown into prison. But she certainly would have enough reasons to do so. Her mother died because of Miaowi's reforms, and based on what Wark told me, she blamed him for not being strong enough to resist Miaowi's power. I heard he even betrothed her to Miaowi's son! She might be angry enough with him to upset his plans.'

'She's right to be angry,' Mia said, surprising Ryan and even herself by taking Karina's side. But if Mia's father had been too weak to protect her mother, she might be angry enough to seek revenge too. Still, that didn't mean she forgave Karina for betraying them. 'Why didn't Wuchiwark at least try to avenge his wife?' she asked.

Wuchichoc shook his head. 'Wark was distraught by his wife's death, but what could we do? Miaowi hadn't meant to kill her, so we couldn't even seek justice. All I could think to do was to try to persuade Miaowi to abandon the new reforms before more people got hurt.'

'I'll bet he didn't,' Mia said dryly.

'He not only didn't, but he also accused me of undermining the council's authority and had me imprisoned.'

'At least he didn't execute you,' Ryan said encouragingly.

'That's because he has even worse plans for me. He wants to get me deported to the Overworld. In fact, one of the reforms he has been trying to implement is to restart the custom of deporting criminals. While most of the councillors have been turning a blind eye to his doings, this is something they strongly object to. It's seen as inhumane, you see, to send people into a chaotic world like yours, where violence and cruelty are so rampant, and even more so since many of us are of the opinion that the day of reckoning is near.'

'Day of reckoning?' Mia echoed.

'The prophecy,' Ryan breathed. 'The end of our world.'

'That's right,' Wuchichoc said. 'The end of your world is near, and unless the prophesied hero rises up, all who live in the Overworld are doomed. So these past ten years, they have been debating back and forth, but Miaowi still can't convince the council to deport me. Meanwhile, I've been left to rot in this prison while awaiting their final decision.' He looked at the grandeur around him sadly, shook his head, and helped himself to a custard bun topped with chocolate chips.

'And your brother? Didn't he try to get you freed?'

'He can't and he shouldn't,' Wuchichoc said between bites. 'If he tried to free me, he would be accused of undermining the council's authority and thrown into prison as well. We couldn't allow that to happen. He must stay outside, so that he can do something about the prophecy. Miaowi doesn't think we should give up the Ef-frock to the hero of the prophecy, even if that hero does appear. He thinks that it's good if everyone in the Overworld is killed, so that we will have a clean slate and the council will no longer object to his plan to deport criminals.'

Wuchichoc paused to choose another pastry from the tray before continuing. 'Of course, that was not all he said to persuade the councillors. He also told them the Ef-frock was too precious a treasure to let it be taken from the Underworld, an argument that few could refute. So, Wark and I agreed that he should lie low and wait till the moment was ripe, then find the hero of the prophecy, or billions of lives would be sacrificed. And your presence here tells me that the time has come, and he has found the hero!'

'The hero …' Mia began, then hesitated, glancing at Ryan. She felt bad about squashing the old man's hope and wondered how she could soften the blow.

'What about him?' Wuchichoc asked eagerly.

Ah well … better to tear off the plaster with a quick rip, Mia thought, so she said flatly, 'He's dead.'

'What!' Wuchichoc choked on his bun and Ryan had to thump him several times on his back. The piece of bread flew across the room and was promptly lost in the thick carpet.

When the old man had recovered, Ryan explained, 'He was struck by lightning.'

The old man stared at him with watery eyes. 'Then … you … you're not Matthew Pane?'

'Our names are Ryan and Mia,' Ryan replied. 'We are the sidekicks. Our friend Julian is the new hero. He's out there right now, somewhere, trying to get the Ef-frock.'

'A new hero …' Wuchichoc murmured. 'Can it really be? But the prophecy was passed down through the ages! It can't be subverted just like that. Tell me, how did Wark find this new hero … this Julian?'

'Julian was there in the right place, at the right time,' Ryan said vaguely, not wanting to undermine his friend's legitimacy with the full story of how he had been chosen at random. 'That's how real heroes come about, don't they?'

'I don't know!' Wuchichoc fretted. 'We haven't had a hero in ages! Haven't had need of one, you know, with things in the Underworld being perfect most of the time. It's only since Miaowi took charge that things started to fall apart. And it's been getting worse. Take this prison, for example. When I was first put in here, I could order room service any time I wanted. Now, meals get served only six times a day, and I only get two trays of snacks to choose from instead of four. Last week, they took away the hot tub, can you imagine! At this rate, I'll bet the hair treatments and manicures will be the next to go.' He used his right hand with its perfectly shaped nails to stroke his long, beautiful hair regretfully.

Ryan became aware that his jaw had dropped during Wuchichoc's rant and quickly snapped it shut.

'Do you know how prisons in the Overworld are like?' Mia could not resist asking.

'What?' the old man said distractedly.

'Sir,' Ryan cut in. 'We have to find a way to escape. Julian needs our help.'

'Not to mention the hairy guard will torture us to death tomorrow morning,' Mia added.

Wuchichoc nodded. 'And he likes to drag out the torture too. No quick and easy death, oh no! He'll make you read the one-starred novels and because they're so boring, you'll take months to finish them, prolonging the agony. You're right. You need to escape. Right now.' He pushed himself upright, whereupon the crumbs on his shirt fell into the plush carpet and disappeared, then walked to the other side of the room. Pulling on a cord, he opened a gap in the curtain, revealing a small door.

'Is that the way out?' Mia breathed, thrilled that their escape was proving to be so easy.

'Oh no,' Wuchichoc said. 'That's the bathroom. "Always use the bathroom before going out," is what my mother used to say. You never know when you'll come upon another.'

The cups of tea had indeed made using the bathroom a necessity for the kids, so they took turns to follow the old man's advice. After they were done (which included gawking at the gold taps, ornate mirrors and scented plush towels), Wuchichoc sat them down again.

'To escape, you need to overpower the guards.'

'How is that even possible?' Mia asked.

Something the hairy guard had said earlier came to Ryan's mind. 'During the torture session, the hairy guard told us there are only four guards on duty in the citadel right now, due to mass food poisoning.'

Wuchichoc nodded. 'That usually happens only about once every two weeks. You're very lucky you were caught at this time. Maybe the prophecy will be fulfilled after all. Now, when there are only four guards on duty, they can usually only spare one for the prison. All we need to do is call for him, then when he opens the door, the three of us can easily overpower him.'

'Great! Then we can go look for Julian!' Ryan said.

Mia looked exasperated. *Relying on Julian again! As if that was any good.* 'We have no idea where he is,' she said coldly. 'Anyway, we shouldn't be wasting time. Since we're already in the citadel, we should head straight up the tower and get the Ef-frock ourselves.'

Ryan thought for a moment, then nodded. 'All right. Julian might already have made his way here anyway. We might just meet him in the tower.'

Wuchichoc looked troubled. 'You know there's a maze in the tower?'

'Yes. The guard told us during the interrogation. But we'll find our way,' Mia said confidently. 'Ryan has a brain of enormous proportions. He'll map out the route in no time.'

Wuchichoc shook his head. 'It's not that easy. The maze is designed in an ingenious way that defies all logic. The only way to solve it is to make your mind go blank instead of trying to devise strategies to conquer the maze. But only the most enlightened Zen monks on the brink of attaining nirvana can clear their minds completely at such a stressful time.'

Mia pursed her lips, a stubborn look on her face. 'We'll figure something out when we get there.'

'And then, there's the other problem,' Wuchichoc continued.

'What other problem?' Ryan asked worriedly.

'It's a bunny.'

'Huh?' Mia said, thinking she had misheard the old man.

'There's a monster in the maze, guarding the treasure. It's a bunny.'

'What's so frightening about a bunny?' Mia asked, frowning.

Wuchichoc dropped his voice and said in an ominous tone, 'It's not just any ordinary bunny.' He paused, a look of barely controlled terror in his eyes. 'It's a really cute one.'

CHAPTER SEVENTEEN

I wasted five minutes trying to decide whether I was more angry or hurt by Karina's disappearance, then gave it up as a lost cause. Karina had clearly tricked me, but I couldn't wrap my mind around it. First, she had betrayed us, leaving us to the city guards—not a surprising move if she was a CATTSS spy. But then she had used me to get into the citadel tower. What was her purpose in doing that? I recalled her terrified expression as we ascended the tower. No, she didn't do that just to spy for the CATTSS. She had wanted to come here, and badly, for some other reason. But what? And if she wasn't a CATTSS spy, then who *was* she?

After thinking hard for a few more minutes, I decided that there was only one reason anyone would take such great risks to come here: the view.

Indeed, as the tallest tower in the entire city, possibly the entire Underworld, the view from the window was breathtaking. I could see the river emerging from under the citadel and follow its flow all the way to the city wall and beyond. The colourful roofs of the city houses and other lesser towers bobbed up at various heights like so many naughty children, giving the view a cheerful carnival-like feel.

I revelled in the sights and, for a moment, forgot all my worries. Faced with such transcendental beauty, the mission to save the world seemed like an irrelevance, the capture of my friends a mere inconvenience, the quest for the Ef-frock a … Eek! The Ef-frock! Karina was here because of the Ef-frock! *Yes, that must be it*, I thought, marvelling at what a piece of work my mind was, to be able to make such complex connections.

The Ef-frock was hidden at the centre of this maze, and it was now a race to see who would get it first. But how would I find my way around? When I had first known about the maze, I had counted on Ryan's intelligence to get us through it. Now that I was alone, how would I figure out the way? Karina was sure to get there before me, if I even got there at all. I started to panic, my heart knocking loudly against my chest wall, further distracting me.

Quick! Think of some maze-solving strategies, I harangued my brain as I began walking down the corridor in front of me. I remembered Ryan mentioning some when we were at Botuni's shop, but no matter how hard I tried, I could not recall a thing. In fact, my brain reacted in exactly the same way as it always did in an exam: it blanked out.

I walked around aimlessly for some time, no concrete plan in place, when suddenly, with no conscious memory of how I had done it, I found myself approaching what must be the centre of the maze, for right there, at the end of a short corridor, was a stone pedestal. And it was empty.

I was too late! Karina had got here before me!

Or perhaps my timing was simply bad and the CATTSS had taken it down for cleaning day.

Just then, a shadow to the left of the pedestal seemed to shift. I realized then that the pedestal was located at a T-junction, and could be approached from three directions. I raced down my passage, turned left, and found Karina lugging a rock the size (and the weight, from the looks of it) of all of Brandon Sanderson's books put together. The stone had an irregular shape, with sharp angles sticking out here and there, and it was glowing alternately red and gold, like an oversized Christmas ornament.

I could just see Karina's face above the huge rock as she pulled at it. She looked as if someone had just stepped on her toes and refused to say sorry.

'Stupid rock!' she cried out in frustration when she saw me. 'Nobody told me it is so big!'

'Yeah … you would think it's something Wuchiwark would have mentioned,' I agreed, rubbing my jaw and studying the famed Ef-frock dubiously. 'How did you even drag it this far?'

'I didn't!' Karina said. 'I pushed it off the pedestal, and it rolled over here. Now I can't even move it one bit! How did you manage to find the way here, anyway?'

'Oh, it wasn't that hard. The maze must be quite small.'

'Small?' Karina said incredulously. 'It took me fifteen minutes to find my way, and I had the help of a map too!'

'I'm not sure a map would help much,' I said. I was really bad at reading maps.

Looking at the enormous rock that lay between us, I said with regret, 'I don't suppose we should work together to carry it, since we're now enemies.'

Karina gave a start, then dropped her hands from the Ef-frock. Her eyes had a steely look in them, and her tone turned defensive as she said, 'I know what you must have thought when you first removed the eye mask and saw that I was gone.'

I asked, surprised, 'You knew that I thought you came here for the view?'

'Is that what you thought?' Karina said, her face softening.

'At first,' I admitted. 'It took me a while to work out that you were after the Ef-frock too. Is that why you offered to help us when we met out on the plains?'

Karina nodded. 'When I heard that my father had asked you to steal the Ef-frock—'

'Your father!' I exclaimed. 'Wuchiwark is your father?'

'Yes.'

'Then you should be on our side!'

'Oh, you don't know the half of it,' Karina said in frustration, flinging herself down to sit against the rock. I edged round the rock and sat beside her, squirming to find a smooth surface to lean on, but the stone seemed to be particularly rough on my side.

'You see,' she said, not noticing my difficulties, 'my mother died shortly after I was born, because of some stupid rule that Miaowi implemented. My father is a weakling. He sits on the council but doesn't dare to do anything to get justice for my mother. He even agreed to betroth me to Miaowi's detestable son!'

'Oof,' I grunted. The sharp points of the rock were digging into my back.

Encouraged by my response, she continued warmly, 'And now Papa has run away to save your world, leaving me behind, all alone. Surely he knows that by doing so, he'll be outlawed, and can never come back. He abandoned my mother to her fate; now he's abandoning me as well! That's why I figured I'll come along with you and grab the Ef-frock first. Then, I'll be able to thwart Papa's plans, and also use the rock as leverage to threaten Miaowi! He must agree to cancel my engagement to Tago, or I'll never give him back the rock!'

'But Miaowi won't allow the Ef-frock to be used to save the Overworld,' I protested, gesticulating wildly and using the motion as a cover for moving my butt around to try to get more comfortable. 'If you give him the stone, my world will die!'

'What else can I do?' Karina said, tearing up. 'You've seen what Tago is like. I can't marry him. I won't!'

'How about letting us use the rock to save my world first, then you can have it to threaten Miaowi?'

'No! Once it's in the hands of my father, he'll never let me use it that way. He'll return the rock to Miaowi and force me to marry Tago to buy peace between himself and the council.'

I could tell that nothing would make her change her mind. Besides, she had already shown very clearly by her actions that she had never regarded us as her friends. 'That's why you betrayed us,' I said sadly, 'and set the CATTSS guards on us.'

Karina's eyes widened. 'What? No, no … I never did that!'

'Then why did you disappear when we arrived at the city?'

'So I could go home and get the map of the maze from my father's study!'

'Why should I believe you?' I challenged.

'It's true!' she insisted. 'You know I would never do anything to harm you. Look, a bunny!'

'Don't try to change the subject,' I said sternly. 'I'm talking about serious matters here.'

'No, I mean it. There's a bunny, over there!'

I turned and when I saw what monstrous animal stood against the far wall of the corridor, I yelped and tried to hide behind Karina.

It was a small, white bunny with a twitchy, pink nose and it stood on its hind legs with its furry ears poised over its head, the ends folded down.

'Oh, it's so cute!' Karina squealed, clasping her hands together.

I cringed behind her, trying hard not to hyperventilate. Images from my childhood flashed before my eyes. A friend's house ... a pet bunny in his yard ... me munching innocently on a carrot ... then the leaping! And the clawing! Oh, how that bunny wanted my carrot! Ever since then, I had had a phobia of these vicious creatures.

'Let's go pat it!' Karina said, taking a step forward.

'No, please!' I begged, clutching her arm.

'I have to!' she said. 'I've never seen such a cute bunny before. Look at its tiny paws! And what dreamy eyes! Its fur must be so soft ...'

She shook off my hand and walked slowly towards the bunny as if trying not to scare it off, though it didn't seem likely to me that such a heartless brute was capable of being scared. I cowered near the Ef-frock, prepared to dash behind it if the bunny so much as took a step forward.

'Karina, come back,' I called desperately.

'In a moment. Just ... need ... to ... pat ... the ... bunny ...' She was very close to it now.

'Are you done?' I asked, my eyes shut tight as I was unable to bring myself to look upon the gruesome scene.

When there was no reply, I opened a slit of an eye and caught sight of Karina disappearing round the corner.

'Hey!' I yelled, leaping to my feet and bounding after her. I turned the corner just in time to see the bunny sink its two huge front teeth into Karina's hand. She gave a startled cry and tried to fling the bunny away from her. At that moment, a rectangular trapdoor beneath her opened and she, together with the animal, dropped into thin air.

'Karina,' I cried, dashing forward. Expecting to see her broken remains lying at the bottom, I was relieved to find instead that she had managed to grip the edge of the hole with both hands. We both watched in horror as the bunny continued to fall at least five storeys down into a pit swarming with hundreds of rabid bunnies, all of them gnashing their fangs and glaring at us viciously with their blood-red eyes. The white bunny's fall was cushioned by its fellows' furry bodies, and it bounded upright to join its friends to hiss and growl at us.

'Help!' Karina gasped.

I knelt down beside the hole and grabbed both her wrists and pulled. Either she was heavier than she looked or the movies made this seem way easier than they should, but no matter how I tugged, I found I didn't have enough strength to pull her up.

'Quickly!' she begged. 'I'm losing my grip!'

I redoubled my efforts, but it was no use. Moreover, the tree branch in my belt kept poking me in the chest, which was most annoying. 'Wait,' I panted, letting go of her wrists. I tugged the branch out of my belt and massaged my bruised chest. *There, much better*, I sighed, turning back to resume my rescue of Karina. But before I could put down the branch to grab her wrists again, her hands slipped and with a scream, she began falling.

What should I do? I thought in a panic. *It's all this branch's fault! If I didn't have to stop to—*

So quick did my mind work that before Karina was even halfway down the shaft, I had finished thinking those two-and-a-half sentences—the last one left incomplete because it occurred then to me that I could use the Krake-rope to save Karina!

Relief and hope swelled within me as I pointed the branch at Karina and shouted, 'Release the Krake-rope!'

It flew with alacrity towards Karina and wound itself securely around her. There! Easy-peasy!

But she continued to fall! I stared at my empty hand in dismay. I had imagined I would pull her up with the rope, but had forgotten to hold on to one end of it! Now, not only did Karina have to fight off hundreds of rabid rabbits, but she had to do it all tied up too!

Kneeling at the edge of the hole, I watched in horror as she landed right in the midst of the murderous creatures. There was no chance she could survive. In a few seconds, she would be ripped to bits! What could I do? What could I do?

Nothing, I realized, falling backwards in shock. *If I close my eyes and don't see it, maybe it won't happen*, I told myself frantically. After all, didn't some great philosopher say that a chair doesn't exist when nobody's looking at it?

But before I could follow my own advice, my attention was drawn towards a loud moan coming from the Ef-frock which had mysteriously moved from its previous position and was now sitting in the corridor behind me.

'No, no, no,' the rock said in tremulous tones. 'I never meant to kill her. It's an accident … no, no, no …'

The Ef-frock could talk? Was it alive? I peered at it in the wavering torchlight and saw something that would have, to anyone else, appeared like blood leaking out from one side of the rock. But I would have recognized that shade of crimson anywhere; I had coveted it for so long. It was the edge of Tago's cloak. The one he was wearing in Botuni's shop.

The rock was not talking. It was Tago—on the other side of the rock.

Grief for Karina's demise blinded me to all sense of caution, and I rushed over to the Ef-frock. Bending down, I reached round the edge of the rock and grasped the ends of the cloak in my hand. 'Come out, you murderer!' I cried as I tugged, trying to pull Tago out of hiding.

To my amazement, the cloak shrank in my hands and vanished, the last folds disappearing into the red-and-gold surface of the rock.

'Not coming out,' the Ef-frock whined in Tago's voice. 'I'm never coming out again!'

'You ... you're trapped inside the Ef-frock?' I asked incredulously.

'Ef-frock is a stupid name, and I refuse to answer to it!' the voice sulked.

It might not be willing to go with you, Wuchiwark had said of the rock, *and it has a bit of a temper ...*

'Oh my ... *you're* the Ef-frock?' I couldn't believe my ears, or my brain, for that matter. Surely I had misread the situation? After all, that was not an infrequent occurrence. In fact, it happened almost all the time.

'I told you I won't answer to that name!' came the petulant response.

'Erm ... Tago?' I asked cautiously.

'That's better,' he said in a slightly mollified tone.

'So, you're a rock and also a human?'

'What? Are you going to discriminate against me because I'm different?'

'No, no ...' I said hastily. 'That's not what I meant at all. Er ... could you come out, please? I feel a bit stupid talking to a rock.'

'Not coming out.'

'Please.'

'Not.'

'Pretty please.'

'Never.'

'I'll give you a cookie.'

There was a slight shimmer of red and gold in the air and then the beautiful rock dissolved into the form of Tago, the handsome but repulsive kid from Botuni's shop. He put out a palm and demanded, 'Cookie.'

Grateful that I had grabbed a jar of 'Auntie Milly's Homemade Cookies' from Botuni's shop as one of the items for my backpack, I now gave him a piece, which he popped into his mouth greedily.

'Who are you, really?' I asked.

'Noch elling ew,' he said with his mouth full, but I noticed he was eyeing the jar in my hands while licking his fingers.

'I'll give you another cookie.'

He snatched it eagerly. 'All right, I'll tell you. I'm a rock spirit.'

'What's that?'

He rolled his eyes at my ignorance but deigned to explain himself: 'Naturally occurring magical objects incubate spirits that will be given human form after several thousand years of existence. My human form came into being thirteen years ago.'

'But how did Miaowi become your father?'

'Cookie.'

I passed him another.

'At the moment of my first transfiguration, Papa and Wuchiwark happened to be present. It was their turn to dust me—in rock form, I mean. You see, the councillors take turns to clean the Ever Rock, since they are the only ones who can navigate the maze. Well, there the two of them were, with their feather dusters, when suddenly, they found themselves dusting a baby instead of a rock. Unsure of what might happen if the news got out, they decided to keep it a secret between them.

Papa pretended I was a baby he'd adopted so that a little boy running around the citadel would not raise suspicions.'

'That's very kind of him,' I said. By then, we were sitting shoulder to shoulder against the wall of the passage and he was helping himself freely to my cookies.

'You think he adopted me out of the kindness of his heart?' Tago snorted. 'He just wants to make use of me. That's why he betrothed me to Karina. He wants to keep his greatest threat close to him.'

'Karina's his greatest threat?' I asked, surprised.

'Not Karina, stupid. Her father, Wuchiwark. Papa wants to be able to keep him under observation. When Wuchiwark disappeared two days ago, Papa ordered me to keep tabs on Karina, in case she knows something of her father's plans. That is why I was at Botuni's shop today. I knew she visits there a lot.'

'So … it was you who betrayed us to the CATTSS guards?' I asked, almost choking on my tears as I realized how I had wronged Karina. And it was too late now to even say I was sorry. I felt as if nothing in the two worlds could cheer me up ever again.

Tago nodded. 'I could see with my X-ray vision—'

'You have X-ray vision? Cool!' I gushed.

'—that you had Overworld clothes in your backpack, so I called my personal quagga, dashed back to the citadel and got your portraits drawn in a jiffy.'

'You have a personal quagga?' I gazed at him adoringly.

Tago drew himself up proudly. 'I am the Ever Rock, the source of all magic in the Underworld. Of course I have my own quagga.'

'Wow! Can you be my new best friend?' I asked. I figured Ryan and Mia wouldn't mind being second and third best. *It's not a competition*, I would tell them sagely. (It was totally a competition. They didn't have X-ray vision or personal quaggas, did they?)

Tago didn't seem to hear me. Instead, his lips trembled and he started to cry. 'I never meant to kill her. I was just jealous of her new friends and wanted you guys caught and tortured to death. When you didn't get caught, I set the bunny loose to lure you to the trap. I didn't expect Karina to be the one to fall in! But it's not my fault. You humans are so fragile,' he complained. 'You die so easily.'

I snapped the cookie jar shut with a suddenness that made Tago jump. Poor Karina! How could I have forgotten about her gruesome death? To think I had wanted this beast to be my best friend! I had even shared with him my cookies made by Auntie Milly! (Whoever she was.) 'Even if you didn't kill Karina on purpose, you did intend to get me and my friends captured,' I said. 'For all I know, they could already be dead!'

Tago leapt to his feet, his face red with anger. 'I owe you no loyalty! Papa took me in and raised me, and taught me everything I know!'

'No wonder you have such bad manners,' I commented.

Tago quivered with barely controlled rage. 'You won't understand! When I was a helpless baby and had no control over my transfiguration yet, Papa took care of me. I'll do whatever he tells me to!'

'Including murdering people?' I asked as I got to my feet because my legs were getting a little numb from sitting too long. However, Tago took a step back, as if threatened by my change in posture.

'I didn't murder anyone!' he said, trembling with emotion. 'All I did was set a bunny loose. And let the guards know there were Overworld spies. And told them what you looked like. I didn't do the killing!'

'It's the same thing,' I said. 'And if you want to redeem yourself, you must come with me. Wuchiwark needs you to save the Overworld.' I flared my nostrils several times to try to relieve an itch inside my nose, but for some inexplicable reason, Tago seemed to take that as a challenge.

'Never!' he cried. 'You can't make me!' And in a swift movement, he had drawn his sword and held it before him in a defensive stance.

'But ... but ... if you don't come with me, all my people will die!' I said, valiantly trying to keep my focus on the conversation despite the persistent itch in my nose, which was becoming quite unbearable.

Perhaps my words had touched his conscience, for a flicker of doubt crossed Tago's face and he lowered his sword by an inch. Relieved, I took advantage of the momentary lull in our repartee to raise my hand to scratch my nose.

In a flash, Tago had taken a step forward and thrust his sword deep into my stomach.

I stared down at the blade in disbelief, one finger still inside my nostril.

'Sorry!' he stuttered, panic written all over his face. 'I thought you were going to hit me!'

Then he pulled out his sword. I gasped at the sudden pain that shot through me and collapsed to my knees. The jar of Auntie Milly's cookies fell from my hand and shattered on the cold, stone floor.

'I didn't know you're allergic to swords!' I heard him say plaintively as I slumped to the ground and darkness closed all around me.

CHAPTER EIGHTEEN

'I don't get it,' Mia said. 'What's so frightening about a very cute bunny?'

Wuchichoc sighed deeply and tugged at his beard. 'The bunny is so cute that nobody can resist going over to pat it. Little do they know that the cuter the rabbit, the more ferocious it is. It will bite your arm off if you're not careful. Also, the bunny in the maze has been trained to lead the unsuspecting to fall through a trapdoor, where you will be torn to pieces by hundreds of the little critters!'

Ryan looked relieved. 'Oh, no fear of that. Julian is terrified of bunnies. Some childhood trauma he had. He'll never want to pat a bunny.'

'How fortuitous,' Wuchichoc murmured. 'Yes, yes … perhaps he is indeed destined to be the one …'

'And now that we know the truth about the bunnies,' Mia interjected, not wanting to indulge the talk about Julian being the destined hero, 'we won't go near them either.'

'Good, good,' Wuchichoc said. 'Now, let's call the guard and you can make your escape.'

'Wait,' Ryan said. 'Aren't you coming with us?'

The old man shook his head. 'Don't you think I could have escaped any time all these past ten years if I wanted to? But if I do, I will become an outlaw. I'll never be able to walk around openly ever again.'

'But,' Ryan protested, 'you do realize that once the prophecy is fulfilled and the Overworld is safe, the council may no longer object to Miaowi's plan to deport criminals?'

Wuchichoc nodded.

'*You* may be deported.'

The old man nodded again. 'But I have faith in Wark. I'm sure he'll clear my name. Besides,' he sighed and looked around him sorrowfully, 'I've got used to the hardships of prison life. No, my young friends, you must leave without me.'

Seeing that Wuchichoc could not be swayed, Ryan reluctantly gave in. The old man went to the door and shouted, 'Anyone out there?'

'Room service has been cancelled!' came a muffled yell from outside.

'No, no! I'm not ordering room service. I need help!'

There were sounds of grumbling, then the peanut guard that the kids had seen earlier unlocked the door. He was tall and muscular and did not look like he could be taken down easily by two kids and an old man.

'What help do you need?' he asked grudgingly.

'It's the carpet,' Wuchichoc whined. 'It hasn't been cleaned in ages! I can't move without stepping on something. Look!' He pulled up one foot while balancing on the other as if he were doing yoga. Indeed, the sole of his foot was encrusted with biscuit crumbs, chocolate stains and goodness knows what else.

'That's what you get for not wearing shoes,' the guard said.

Wuchichoc looked aghast. 'Only barbarians wear shoes in their house!'

The guard sighed. 'All right. Wait here.' He left the cell and returned half a minute later with a brush and a dustpan. Getting down on his knees, he said, 'I wish they had not outlawed the use of magic in the citadel. Just one small sticker and the carpet will be clean in no time. It's such a—'

He never got to complete the sentence as Wuchichoc had picked up the tray of pastries and smashed it down on his head. Butter cakes and chocolate eclairs flew all over the room, and the guard slumped down to the carpet.

'Oh dear ... now he has even more to pick up when he wakes,' Wuchichoc fretted. 'Well, it can't be helped.'

'Will you get into trouble for helping us escape?' Ryan asked worriedly.

'Oh no,' the old man chuckled. 'It's forbidden to punish me while the council is still deliberating my sentence. It's been like this for ten years! You two should go though. There's no law protecting you.'

'We should see if we can find our backpacks,' Ryan suggested.

'Good idea,' Mia said.

Wuchichoc accompanied the kids out of the cell, and they found the backpacks hanging on a hook near the stairs. Mia was already putting on her backpack when she saw that Ryan was standing motionless.

'What's the matter?' she asked.

Ryan looked up, a slow smile spreading across his face. 'Remember Julian's last words to us?'

Mia clicked her tongue in irritation. 'What?'

'He said, "take all the plush pillows". I finally figured out what that means!'

'He was delirious? Insane? Plain stupid?'

'No!' Ryan took Mia by her arm and hurried her back into the cell, with Wuchichoc trotting behind them, cracking some peanuts he had picked up along the way.

'Look!' Ryan said, pointing to the plump pillows in their white linen cases, stacked neatly on the oversized beds. 'Plush pillows!'

Mia rolled her eyes. 'You don't mean to say Julian wants us to take them?'

'Absolutely!' Ryan said, putting his backpack down on the tea table, which was now conveniently cleared of the snack tray. 'Got to get rid of some dead weight to make space for the pillows,' he said. Each of the items in his bag had been carefully selected at Botuni's shop but now he threw them out with reckless abandon, keeping only his Overworlder clothes. There was a necklace that protected the wearer from poison, a salve that healed all serious wounds, a hat that deflected lightning and a pen that was also a sword. He didn't know how that last item worked, but he supposed it would be quite deadly to stab the nib into someone's eye.

As Ryan proceeded to stuff pillows into his backpack, he urged, 'Come on, Mia. You got to help. I can only fit five into my backpack.'

'No way!' Mia protested.

Ryan stopped his work for a moment to affix Mia with a serious look. 'It was Julian's last words. Although I still haven't worked out why he needs them, we can't let him down.'

'You probably misheard,' Mia said crossly. 'I thought it sounded more like 'marshmallows'.'

Ryan looked exasperated. 'Which makes more sense to you? Pillows or marshmallows?'

'Both sound like utter rubbish to me,' she muttered.

'Go with the flow,' Wuchichoc interjected peaceably, picking up a pillow and shoving it into Mia's arms. 'Since it means so much to Ryan, what's the harm in letting him have his way?'

Mia looked at the two of them and finally threw her backpack on the table in a huff. 'I give up! Let's pack the pillows and go. We've wasted enough time already!' She upended the backpack and out came weapons of various potencies, from crossbows to daggers to battle axes.

Fortunately, the kids had no problem fitting five large, fluffy pillows into each of the small, standard-issue adventurer's backpacks. Their own Overworlder clothes took up the sixth space. Armed with ten pillows, they were finally ready to leave the dungeon.

'There will still be three guards in the citadel,' Wuchichoc warned. 'Two will be guarding the front and back entrances, leaving one to patrol inside the citadel. Be very careful and take no chances.'

'Thank you,' Ryan said gratefully, feeling rather sorry that he had to leave the old man in prison. 'We won't forget all the help you've given us.'

'We'll tell your brother we met you,' Mia added. 'Hopefully, he'll be able to clear your name soon.'

'Oh, tell him to take his time,' Wuchichoc said. 'No hurry at all.'

On that cheerful note, the kids said goodbye and Wuchichoc closed the cell door with a proprietary air as if it were the front door of his own house. The kids walked down the passageway, passed the two torture chambers (shuddering at the memory of what lay behind one of them) and proceeded up the stairs. They moved as quietly as they could, pausing every now and then to listen for the tell-tale footfalls of a patrolling guard.

'I suppose if we encounter a guard, we'll suffocate him with a pillow,' Mia said sarcastically, still seething inwardly that she had been forced to give up all her powerful weapons.

'Good idea,' Ryan said, pulling out a pillow from his bag and clutching it in front of him.

'Are you crazy?' Mia asked incredulously.

'Shh!' Ryan replied. They had reached the ground level and could see the passage that led to the kitchen on their right. 'We'll go the other way,' he said after ascertaining there was nobody around.

The kids crept out of the stairwell and scampered down the corridor, hoping no one would come out of the kitchen and see them. Fortunately, the citadel seemed deserted. When Mia expressed surprise, Ryan reminded her, 'People in the Underworld don't work overtime. Hopefully, everyone has gone home by now.'

They went through an archway and into a spacious, vaulted hall that looked like a conference or dining room, for there was a large, elongated table in the centre, surrounded by several dozen chairs. Seven other arched doorways framed the two longer sides of the room.

'Which way now?' Mia asked in dismay.

Ryan thought for a bit. 'We'll see which doorway has stairs leading up.'

Not daring to wander around the CATTSS' fortress alone, they went together to check out each archway. All seemed to lead into smaller rooms, beyond which they could see more corridors. 'The citadel is too huge,' Mia groaned. 'It'll take us ages to explore which doorway is the right one.'

'A wise person once said, when in doubt, use "eeny meeny miny moe",' Ryan said.

Mia snapped, 'Great, snaking walls! Julian is *not* a wise person and that is the stupidest idea I've ever heard.'

'Any ideas then how to decide which doorway to take?' Ryan asked mildly.

Two minutes later, they stood at the foot of a flight of spiral stone stairs, wondering how long it would take them to get to the top.

'Just because it worked this time doesn't mean it's a good idea,' Mia muttered, half-annoyed that they had found the stairwell so easily using Ryan's proposed method.

The staircase went round and round, rising in a wide circle that hugged an inner column. Every now and then, the monotony of the evenly-spaced steps would be broken by a small landing where the kids could rest (Ryan's pillow came in very handy here as a cushion) and gaze out of a small, vertical arrow slit in the stone wall to check their progress.

'We're really high up,' Ryan said nervously when they had reached their third or fourth landing. He felt his tummy doing somersaults and moved away from the slit nervously, even though he knew it was impossible to fall out from such a small opening.

'At least we're taking the stairs,' Mia said. 'Imagine what it would be like if we had to climb the tower from the outside.'

Ryan agreed that such an act would be borderline psychotic and that nobody in their right mind would attempt it.

The kids continued their ascent, and after what seemed like a century and a half, they reached a landing where there was a solid wooden door, reinforced with metal, on the inner side of the circular stairwell.

'Do you think the maze is in there?' Ryan whispered.

Mia hesitated. Beyond the landing, the stairs continued upwards. 'We're not yet at the top,' she said.

Ryan put his hand on the bolt. 'I think we should check it out anyway.' From the way the steps curved gradually instead of sharply, he could tell that they were circling an extremely large core—certainly large enough to contain a maze. He pulled back the bolt and swung the door open.

There was no maze, only a huge circular cell with an extremely high ceiling.

And it was filled with snarling, snapping bunnies. Those nearest the door turned to look at Ryan, a wild, hungry look in their eyes.

'Yikes!' Ryan yelped, throwing his pillow at them just as they leapt towards him.

The bunnies fell upon the pillow and, within seconds, reduced it to shreds. Feathers burst out of the case and descended on the creatures like drifts of snow.

Ryan was about to slam the door shut when Mia spotted something and cried out, 'Wait!'

Through the cloud of feathers, they saw a large bundle fall from above and on the swarming mass of moving bodies.

'Ouches!' Karina gasped as she landed, though she did not seem hurt. Not yet, anyway. Her fall had been cushioned by the soft bodies of the rabbits. For some strange reason, she was wrapped from neck to shin in rope, and was now trying to keep her head and feet in the air while the bunnies clawed and bit at her bindings.

'Karina!' Ryan yelled.

Karina turned her head and when she saw them, cried out with relief, 'Help me!'

'Why should we help a traitor?' Mia demanded.

'Can we save the philosophical discussions for later?' Karina asked, struggling to keep her unprotected body parts away from the grasping bunnies.

'Roll yourself over,' Ryan suggested, throwing another pillow at the bunnies to keep them from pouncing at him and Mia.

'I can't!' Karina panted. 'I can barely keep myself from being eaten!' Already, the bunnies had chewed partway through the ropes. Fortunately, a large number of them were distracted by the pillow and were fighting with each other to get to the new treat.

'The pillows!' Mia cried, pulling urgently on the drawstring of her backpack. 'We can make a path for Karina using the pillows!'

'Yes, yes!' Ryan replied excitedly.

Mia hurled a pillow towards the centre of the room just as the bunnies broke through Karina's rope bindings, freeing her. Karina hopped on to the pillow, wobbling precariously as the bunnies tore through the case from below. Mia and Ryan threw pillow after pillow, allowing Karina to cross the room using a combination of hops, crawls and lunges, leaving behind her a trail of feathery destruction that resembled a snowstorm in a polar vortex.

Reaching the door at last, she fell into Mia's arms. Ryan threw their last pillow into the room to block off the rabbits, then slammed the door shut. He heaved the bolt across the door just in time, for the kids could hear the thunks on the wood as the rabbits hurled themselves at the door.

Karina sank to the floor, hugging herself tight and quaking from her narrow escape.

Mia regarded her coldly for a moment, then said, 'So, what is Wuchiwark's daughter doing here?'

Karina blinked. 'You know?'

'We met your uncle in the dungeon that you had us thrown into.'

'It wasn't—' Karina began, then broke off. 'We've no time for that. Julian is up in the maze with the Ef-frock and might be in danger. I fell into a trap meant for him, I think.'

'We can question Karina later,' Ryan said to Mia, impatient to continue up the tower now that he knew for certain that Julian was there.

Mia considered the possibility that Karina was leading them into a trap, but then her ordeal with the bunnies seemed real enough. 'All right,' she said grudgingly at last.

With Karina in the lead, the kids resumed their trek up the stairs, this time with the certainty that they would soon reach the top, but also with great trepidation, for they had run out of pillows, which was a very dangerous situation to be in.

Fortunately, they met with neither guards nor more bunnies, and after several minutes, the steps terminated at a very last landing, where a door banded with iron, similar to the one below, greeted them.

Mia drew back the bolt and they stepped into a stone passage. With Karina leading the way, they advanced slowly towards the centre of the maze. Despite having a map, the maze was so confusing with identical-looking passages and corners that the kids made several wrong turns before finally finding their way. As they neared the centre, they could make out muffled voices that sounded like an argument was taking place.

'Quick!' Karina said, starting to run. Mia and Ryan followed. The voices, distorted by the echoes of the maze, sounded strangely ominous. But if the sounds frightened the kids, the silence that suddenly fell upon the maze was even more terrifying. Why had the voices stopped? What was going on?

They quickened their steps as they rounded the last corner, only to jostle into Karina, who had suddenly stopped short.

'What? What?' Mia demanded, her view blocked by Karina.

Mia stepped to one side so she could look over Karina's shoulder, then wish she hadn't, for she saw that they were too late. Sprawled on his back, in front of a gigantic, luminous rock, was Julian—the stand-in hero of the age-old prophecy. A red stain that was still expanding marked the front of his white shirt like a bull's eye, and beside him was a bloody sword and a smashed jar of Auntie Milly's cookies.

Part - III

CHAPTER NINETEEN

I groaned. Or tried to anyway, for my throat seemed to have closed up. How much time had passed since I blacked out? It could have been hours, maybe even days. My eyelids felt heavy; I couldn't seem to open them. I tried to get up, but my limbs were numb, my body leaden. I was paralysed! The sword must have severed my spine or something like that. The shock of that realization would have made me shoot to my feet, except that I could not move at all.

There was an annoying buzz in my ear, but I couldn't even lift my hand to swipe away the insect. I was certain I had lost a great deal of blood, for I felt faint and weak. Was I still bleeding? I couldn't tell, having lost all feeling in my body. *It's a good thing*, I consoled myself. *At least I can't feel any pain. It's a good way to die.*

The buzz was growing louder and more distinct. Gradually, it resolved itself into the sounds of people talking. Their voices sounded familiar … wait, was that Mia crying? And Ryan stammering his disbelief at my fate? There was a third voice, but it couldn't be … how could it be? Karina was dead, mauled to death by cute, little bunnies.

'Don't be silly!' the voice was telling Mia and Ryan. 'What are you crying for?'

It *was* Karina! She was alive! Relief surged through me, to be abruptly replaced by indignation. What was so silly about weeping for me? *She* was the hard-hearted one, not to drop a single tear. Although we had only known each other for a day, we had braved untold dangers together and exchanged eye masks. Surely I deserved some grieving from her? I, at least, had mourned her for several minutes before getting distracted by Tago the Ef-frock's awesomeness. Who, by the way, after initial overtures of friendship, had murdered me. Wow. It was probably a good thing I was almost dead. If I lived to grow up, I was sure to develop all sorts of complexes as a result of all these acts of betrayal.

'He … he's dead,' Ryan blubbered. 'We have failed. The quest is over!'

'He's not dead,' Karina retorted. 'He's just having an allergic reaction.'

'Allergic reaction?' Mia repeated, sounding stupefied.

Allergic reaction? Ah, I see. Karina wasn't hard-hearted after all. She was merely in denial. Her brain could not accept the fact that I was dead and thus conjured up an alternative explanation.

'Yes, see this red stain on his shirt?' Karina said. 'It's because of that sword.'

'Obviously.' That was Mia, sarcastic even in the face of profound grief.

'I recognize the sword,' Karina said. 'It's Tago's.'

Oh, good! They've identified the owner of the weapon! Now they will be able to avenge me!

Karina continued, 'Miaowi bought it for him. It used to be a popular toy in the Underworld.'

Some toy! Sharp enough to kill!

There was a light clattering sound, then a few clicks. 'See? The top half of the blade retracts when you stab with it, and artificial blood spews out of the hidden grooves. The toy was recalled some time back by the manufacturer because they discovered some people are severely allergic to the artificial blood, but Tago refused to give it up.'

'So ... he's not dead?' Ryan asked, his voice edged with hope.

'Of course not!' Karina snorted. It sounded like she was rummaging in her backpack, then my lips were prized open and a few drops of liquid fell into my mouth.

'What's that?' Mia asked suspiciously.

'Anti-allergy potion.'

'What a useful thing to carry with you!' Ryan said admiringly.

'Of course,' Karina replied. 'I never go on a quest without it.' There was a pause, then she asked, voice tinged with curiosity, 'What do you Overworlders bring on quests? I haven't seen any of you with anything useful so far.'

'Well, Overworlders generally don't go on quests,' Ryan said defensively. Then, he added with a touch of pride, 'But we did bring the pillows that Julian wanted.'

I wanted? Since when had I wanted pillows? Although, now that the numbness was dissipating, I was beginning to feel the uncomfortable hardness of the stone floor under my head. *A pillow would be nice*, I thought, and waited for Ryan to take one out for me.

'And don't say they're useless because we used them all to save you from the bunnies!' Mia added provocatively.

So, no more pillows left for me? I felt strangely sad. My life had been touched by so many disappointments lately.

But Karina's next words both surprised and moved me. 'It was Julian?' She sounded so tender, so grateful. 'Then he's saved me twice. When I fell into the trap, he was so resourceful and quick-thinking. If he hadn't tied me up with the Krake-rope, the bunnies would have bitten me straightaway. And now you say the pillows were also his idea ...'

'I don't mind taking credit for that,' I tried to say, although what came out was more like, 'Aye wo why ach-eng air-e or air.'

'He mumbled!' Ryan said joyfully. 'The potion must be taking effect!'

'Death is too good for him,' Mia said, though her voice sounded strangely muffled as if she was fighting back tears.

After a minute, I was able to open my eyes and then sit up. Ryan threw himself at me in an attempt to hug me, promptly knocking me down to the ground again in my weak state. 'Sorry, sorry,' he said, as he and a beaming Mia helped me up.

While waiting for me to recover fully, Mia and Ryan recounted what had happened to them since their capture. Karina then spoke about our own adventures, with me adding in a word here and there when I felt she had not sufficiently conveyed the heroic aspects of our journey.

'So are you on our side or not?' Mia demanded when story time was over.

'I am now,' Karina said, looking at me. 'I owe you for saving my life. I'll help you bring the rock to my father.'

'But what about your betrothal to Tago?' I asked.

'I'll find another way to cancel it,' she said with a resolute lift of her chin.

'Not cancelling it!' came Tago's voice from within the stone, but we all ignored him.

Ryan looked around nervously. 'We should get out of the citadel, before the guards find us.'

'What about the Ef-frock?' Mia asked. She looked at the rock critically, as if measuring it with her eyes, then turned to me. 'It looks way too heavy for us to lift. Can you get Tago to transform?'

'He only comes out for cookies,' I informed her regretfully.

'I'm not eating cookies contaminated with glass shards!' Tago warned.

'I'll pick out most of them,' Ryan offered.

'Not coming out!'

Karina sighed. 'It's no use. I know Tago. He's so stubborn, he'll never budge. We're stuck.'

I was just thinking of asking whether there was an oven (and some flour, sugar, eggs and chocolate chips) in the citadel that we could use when Ryan said with uncharacteristic confidence, 'No, we're not.' He walked over to the Ef-frock, opened his standard-issue adventurer's backpack, and popped the rock in. 'See?' he said triumphantly. 'Not stuck at all.'

Was it my imagination or did Ryan appear more confident than he had been before? He must have been inspired by my awesome leadership abilities.

After everyone (except Tago, who yelled 'kidnapper!' from the backpack) had congratulated Ryan for being a genius, we considered our next move.

'There are three guards left in the citadel,' Ryan said. 'Wuchichoc said only one will be guarding the back entrance and one the front. We can try going out through the back. Hopefully, they posted their weaker guard there.'

'There's four of us anyway,' Mia said. 'Surely we can take down one guard.'

Ryan, Karina and I agreed that Mia could certainly take down one guard while the rest of us served as lookouts. With that settled, Ryan said, 'Karina, please guide us back to the tower staircase with your map.'

'I've a better idea,' Karina said. 'Julian can guide us. He's a maze prodigy! He found the centre in half the time I did, without a map!'

'He did?' Mia asked disbelievingly. 'Wuchichoc said the maze is virtually uncrackable.'

'Show her!' Karina told me.

'Er …' I said.

'Show her!' Karina said again, more insistently, while staring defiantly at Mia.

In a rare burst of clarity, I realized I was a helpless pawn caught in a battle of pride between two headstrong girls. To buy myself some time, I took a few tentative steps down the passage, pretending to examine the turnings. It had been a total fluke that I found the centre of the maze. I had been so stressed out that I hadn't even been thinking straight! But how could I admit that to my friends? They would think poorly of me and lose confidence in their leader. What should I do? Perhaps I could peek at Karina's map? No, that would show me up as not just a loser but also a cheat. I had led my sidekicks too far on this adventure to let them down now. If only I could remember the turnings I took earlier! But even if I could, that would lead us to the window, not the stairs. Oh, this was hopeless. My mind was a total blank.

'See?' Karina said. 'Told you.'

Somehow, without my realizing it, I had found the way to the stairs with my friends trailing quietly behind me.

Mia opened her mouth, and I waited for her customary snide remark, but she shut it again without saying a word. To my surprise, I noticed that the way she looked at me had changed. Instead of impatience and mockery, I saw approval and respect.

'Good job, Ju!' Ryan exclaimed, clapping me on my back.

I mumbled something about luck, which only served to raise my friends' esteem of me even higher. *Not just brilliant, but modest too!* they signalled to each other with their looks. At least, I was pretty certain that was what they were trying to say.

We hurried down the steps as fast as our legs could carry us, which in my case was not very fast, for my legs were still a little wobbly from my earlier ordeal. Pausing about halfway down the tower to let me rest, Mia happened to glance out of an arrow slit. 'Marauding dragon!' she exclaimed.

'Where?' Karina asked in alarm.

I patted her arm reassuringly. 'Don't worry. There is no dragon. It's just the way Mia swears. She believes she's the reincarnation of a medieval king and—'

'No!' Mia interrupted. 'There really is a marauding dragon outside. Look!'

We all squeezed beside her and squinted out of the narrow gap in the wall. Far below us, a large contingent of guards could be seen shepherding a huge dragon into the courtyard at the back of the fortress. Even from the distance, we could make out the snapping jaw on the fearsome head and the formidable wingspan of the mythical creature as it stretched its limbs.

'I thought Wuchichoc said there are only three guards left to guard the citadel!' Ryan gasped.

Tago's sulky voice could be heard from inside Ryan's backpack. 'When the rabbit trap was activated, a message was automatically transmitted to my father that there are intruders in the citadel. He must have deployed the city guards to come to the defence of the citadel.'

'And you're only telling us now?' Karina huffed, shaking her fist at Ryan's bag.

The dragon was now sitting on its haunches, its massive body taking up almost all the available space in the yard, obediently awaiting its instructions.

I shook my head. 'And they have a problem with quaggas taking up too much parking space in the city?'

Mia said in dismay, 'The front entrance will be similarly guarded, I'm sure. What should we do now?'

Ryan looked thoughtful. 'Remember when we were being tortured by the hairy guard, he mentioned something about the cellar grate being damaged by rust?'

Mia nodded excitedly. 'He said it leads to the river!'

'The river runs through the citadel,' Karina piped up. 'If we can get out by the grate, we can follow the river out to the city wall!'

Feeling slightly more hopeful, we started down the staircase again. Soon, we reached a corridor and exited it via an archway, finding ourselves in a spacious, vaulted hall with seven other arched doorways.

'Which archway do you think leads to the cellar?' Mia asked.

'Eeny meeny ...' I began.

'This way!' Karina cut in, pointing to the one directly opposite us. 'I've been in the citadel a few times with my father. I think I remember the way.'

The rest of us trooped after her as she led us down another long flight of stairs—nowhere near as long as the tower stairs, but I was feeling quite exhausted by then and every step felt like ten.

Finally, we reached the end and stepped out into a great, yawning cave. As with the rest of the citadel, a few torches had been left burning in brackets on the wall, and we were able to see that the place had been made over into some sort of a library. Bookcases lined the uneven stone walls and each shelf was laden with tome after tome of leather-bound books.

'They use their cellar to store books?' Ryan said, impressed. He walked over to a shelf and ran his fingers over their spines, pulling out books here and there at random to look at their covers.

'This isn't the cellar,' Karina said in dismay. 'I must have remembered wrong. I should have taken the archway next to this one.'

'Wow!' Ryan said, totally oblivious to Karina's revelation. 'This book teaches you how to brew potions! And this one tells you all about quagga-rearing!'

Mia had walked round the room looking for hidden passageways, and had not found any. 'Distressing damsels! Now's not the time to get all book-wormy,' she chastised. 'We'll have to backtrack to the hall, all because our dear friend here got it wrong.'

The thought of having to climb up all those stairs that I had had so much trouble coming down was discomfiting, to say the least. 'Are you sure it's not wiser,' I asked wistfully, 'to just wander around here for a few hours, and hope we might come upon an alternate route?'

'Of course not!' Mia said, pulling me with her as she headed for the stairs, whereupon my knees gave way beneath me and I sank to the floor like a puddle of jelly.

'What's wrong with you?' she said in surprise.

'I'm a puddle of jelly,' I said mournfully.

Karina squatted in front of me and peered into my face. 'He does look rather pale. Probably tired out from the allergic reaction he had earlier.'

'Can't you give him more of that anti-allergy potion?' Ryan asked, leaving the shelves to come over and look at me. I was beginning to feel like a zoo exhibit.

Karina shook her head. 'It won't be of any use. He's already cured of the allergy. He's just tired.'

'But we don't have time to let him rest!' Mia said.

'Can we magic out a flying carpet for him or something?' Ryan suggested. 'I've still got one sticker left.'

Karina bounced to her feet excitedly. 'You've got a sticker? We can't magic out something from nothing, but we can use a sticker to help him regain his strength!'

Ryan put away the book he was still holding to free up his hands, then took out our last sticker: a Level Four.

'This is a simple spell,' Karina said. 'A Level Four should be more than enough. Too bad we don't have any more stickers for dealing with the dragon, if it does come to that.'

Ryan blanched and quickly put his hands behind his back, hiding the sticker. 'Maybe we should save this for the dragon.'

'Then what do we do with him?' Karina pointed at me. I had slumped to the floor completely at this point, having decided to do what zoo animals usually did when there were visitors—lie on the ground and drowse. I think I might even have drooled a little.

Eventually, the three of them decided they could neither carry nor leave me, the hero of the adventure, behind. So, Ryan reluctantly gave up the sticker. Karina lifted my shirt and pasted it on my stomach, saying, 'Give him strength!'

Within seconds, I felt a warmth spark in my belly, simmer for a bit, then spread in a burst throughout my body. I sprang to my feet and danced a caper. I couldn't help it! I felt awash in energy.

'Let's go!' I cried, bounding up the stairs easily, then ran down the flight of stairs in the neighbouring corridor and back up again while waiting for my friends to reach the hall.

When they arrived, I said, 'That's the way to the cellar all right—I've checked!' then skipped down the corridor ahead of them.

'Too bad we didn't have a less powerful sticker,' Karina muttered, running to keep up.

'I can't believe we wasted our last sticker on that,' Ryan agreed regretfully.

The cellar was another cave, but much bigger and deeper than the previous one. The citadel had evidently been built over a network of natural caverns, which the CATTSS had made over into rooms. Crates and barrels lined the sides of this one, leaving a wide passage in the middle that took us, after a minute or two, to a rocky outcrop where the river swept past before us. In the direction of the river flow, there was indeed a large grille gate formed of bars secured into the surrounding stone. The part where the water was constantly sloshing over was reddish-brown with rust. A couple of bars had even completely disintegrated, the broken parts long washed away. It certainly looked like a viable escape route.

There was just one problem. Sitting next to the grate, at the edge of the outcrop, was a beefy-looking citadel guard with muscles rippling through the tight cloth of his red-and-gold livery. In his hands was a bunch of tree branches fanned out like a bouquet, and he was pointing them directly at us.

CHAPTER TWENTY

'Release the Krake-ropes!' the guard intoned in a deep, bass voice. Four sinuous branches shot out from among the cluster in his hand and twined themselves around us.

'I've got you now,' he rumbled, leaning over our fallen bodies and flexing his formidable biceps.

'No, you haven't!' I shouted, tensing my own muscles in readiness to burst out of my flimsy binds. I felt like Popeye on an overdose of spinach, my whole body radiating strength.

'Yes, I have,' the guard insisted with the air of someone who enjoyed a good debate.

'Then you're wrong!' I said, straining against the ropes.

'I'm not,' he said.

'You are!'

'Am not.'

'Oh yeah, you're not,' I admitted, panting and finally giving up on breaking the unyielding ropes.

'Told ya!' the guard said triumphantly.

'You can't defeat a Level Six magical item with magic from a Level Four sticker, stupid,' came Tago's sour voice from inside Ryan's backpack.

'Who said that?' the guard said, flinching and glaring all around suspiciously.

'Nobody,' said Tago.

'I heard that!' the guard snapped. 'It came from you!' He squatted down in front of Ryan and grabbed him by his ropes, lifting him bodily with one hand.

'It wasn't me!' Ryan squeaked.

'It was!'

'Wasn't!'

'Was—oomph!'

Ryan thumped back down on the stone floor as the guard flew across the cavern, knocked his head against a crate and fell down unconscious.

'Well done, Ju!' Mia crowed. I smiled in appreciation of her praise. So what if I couldn't break out of the ropes? My legs had the strength of ten lions. When the guard had lowered himself to grab Ryan, he had put his body within the range of my feet and one kick from me had done the trick.

'MIRE will get us out of these ropes in no time,' Karina announced.

'No, I can't!' Mia said sharply. 'Are you trying to set me up?'

'I meant M-I-R-E, Miss Prickly,' Karina said. 'Magical Influence Remover Emollient. I've got a bottle in my backpack, but I can't reach it.'

She wriggled about until she was lying on her stomach. Her backpack revealed itself as a lump under the ropes. I rolled over to her side and, despite being tied up from shoulder to shin, rose to an upright sitting position using my ultra-strong core muscles. Then, I began forcing Karina's ropes apart with the tips of my power-laced fingers that were fortunately outside of my bindings. After some effort, I managed to make a big enough gap between the coils to open her backpack and take out the bottle of MIRE. In a few moments, I had turned the ropes back into tree branches and freed all of us.

Mia took one of the branches and stalked over to the guard. 'Release the Krake-rope!' she commanded, her lips curling with relish at getting her revenge. Once the guard was securely bound, we proceeded to inspect the rusty gate. The gap was too small for us to squeeze through, but I flexed my muscles and snapped off a couple more bars, and soon all of us were through without any difficulty. The water was only slightly chilly, and reached up to our waist as we wadded along the dark tunnel. At Karina's suggestion, I took the opportunity to wash off the fake blood from my shirt. The pinprick of light at the end of the tunnel assured us of a way out, and we made our way towards it, aided by the gentle current.

The tiny glow grew larger as we approached it, and in time, we saw that another set of grilles barred our exit at the end. That hardly served as an obstacle for me though, and we got through easily, the grate now a tangled mess of iron behind us.

There were houses and other buildings on both sides of the river and occasionally someone walked by, but fortunately, nobody seemed to have seen us climbing out of the water. It was hard to look respectable while dripping wet, so we made loud remarks to each other about how unlucky we were to have fallen into the river by accident. We figured that we would appear less suspicious that way, and we must have been right, for no one paid us any notice.

The tunnel had taken us half a mile out from the citadel, and after we had walked another half a mile, we felt relatively safe from the guards and dragon that were still staking out the citadel. The plan was to continue following the river until we were two miles south of the citadel, whereupon we would call our quaggas to take us to the southern gate. We would then have to find a way past the guards before we could call on our faithful steeds again to take us back to the field where the secret entrance to the Overworld was located.

'Why can't we just get our quaggas to take us through the city gates?' Ryan asked. 'They can zip past so quickly the guards won't even know we were there.'

Karina shook her head. 'Quaggas are the most law-abiding creatures in the world. They will insist on stopping at the gates for inspection. And then they will look so nervous and shifty that they'll end up giving us away. No, it's better not to have them with us at the gates.'

'Could we have *them* instead?' I asked, pointing to two figures sitting by the riverbank, their legs dangling over the edge of the promenade.

'The Soothy sisters!' Karina exclaimed joyfully, quickening her steps to meet our old friends.

'Matthew!' they cried, rising up to come towards us.

Mia looked at me quizzically, and I blushed. 'Oh yeah, I forgot to tell her the hero of the prophecy has been replaced,' I said sheepishly.

'Are you ever going to tell them?' she asked.

'I will, some day. But they're such great fans of the prophecy, I'll hate to burst their bubble …' I broke off as the sisters came up to us.

After introducing Mia, Ryan and the Soothies to each other, Big Soothy demanded, 'Have you done it?'

'Yes,' I said proudly.

The sisters whooped with joy, throwing up their hats and cavorting about the promenade. 'The CATTSS have been overthrown!' they shouted. 'The evil reign is over!'

'Shh!' I urged, hunching my shoulders in an attempt to make myself disappear and glancing around nervously. A few passers-by had stopped in their tracks to stare at us curiously.

'There's nothing to be afraid of now that the CATTSS are gone!' Small Soothy whooped.

'But they haven't been overthrown!' I hissed.

The Soothies looked shocked, their limbs frozen in mid-dance.

'But you said you've done it!' Big Soothy accused.

'I meant I'd succeeded in stealing the Ef-frock,' I said, and seeing the disappointment washing over their faces, added quickly, 'which means we're halfway to overthrowing the CATTSS.'

It took a while for the sisters to process this logic, but they eventually did, and broad smiles spread over their open, friendly faces.

'You're right, Matthew,' Small Soothy said. 'So what's your plan now?'

'We need to get the Ef-frock to our friend, who will know what to do,' I said.

'That's a vague plan,' Big Soothy said approvingly.

'Sounds vague to me,' Small Soothy agreed.

Ryan and Mia, who had wisely been staying out of the dubious conversation I had been having so far, now plucked at my sleeves.

'City guards!' Ryan whispered. I turned and saw a whole army of brown-and-green liveried men striding down the street in our direction. Every now and then, one or two would detach from the main group to question a pedestrian, or charge into a side street.

'They've discovered we've escaped from the citadel!' Karina gasped.

'Ow, ow, ow!' I cried.

'Are you all right?' Ryan asked anxiously.

'Yeah,' I said. 'Just checking to see if my quagga would come, but I guess we're still too near the city centre.'

'The guards are headed our way,' Mia said. 'They'll find us in a moment!'

'Especially since we're standing out here on the promenade in full view,' I agreed.

'And also,' added Karina, 'because those people over there who had been staring at us just tipped the guards off.'

Indeed, a couple of civilians had their heads together with the captain of the guards at that very moment. The captain looked up, gave a shout and pointed his tree branch in our direction.

'Go!' Big Soothy commanded. 'We'll help to create a distraction.'

There was no time to ask them questions or refuse their offer several times before accepting reluctantly. We gave the sisters our heartfelt thanks, then made off down the river. After a while, we noticed that the people in front were rushing by us, excited looks on their faces.

'… rare street performance of the Soothy Sisters' Spectacular Stunt Show …' we overheard a man saying as he hurried past.

Turning around, we glimpsed, through the gathering crowd, the two sisters juggling fire hoops while barbecuing turkey legs. The audience was swelling by the second and soon the entire street, including the promenade area, was blocked by the cheering spectators.

'Oh, I love their show!' Karina gushed. 'Can't we stay to watch until it's over?'

'Okay!' I said, not taking my eyes off the mesmerizing performance.

'No!' Mia said firmly, pulling us away.

Reluctantly, and with much nostalgia for the turkey legs that I had gobbled down earlier today, I turned and followed my friends down the river.

If they had not been running so fast, and if they had not been belting out 'la-la-la-la' and covering their ears so they could not hear my pleas to stay for the show, I could have told them that there was no point in running, for out of the corner of my eye, I had seen a great shadow fall over the citadel's spire in the distance.

The dragon had arisen, and it was coming straight for us.

CHAPTER TWENTY-ONE

'Awesome Mia, awesome Mia,' Mia kept muttering as we ran along the river.

Humility had never been my strong point but this seemed rather excessive even to me. She must have chanted the phrase about twenty times as we ran along the river when there was a sudden gust of wind, and a brown quagga with white legs appeared beside us.

'Hello, Mia,' she said. 'Where to?'

'Great! We're far enough from the city centre now,' Mia said to us. 'Quick, call your quaggas too!'

'Your code phrase is "awesome Mia"?' Karina snickered.

'So? What's yours?' Mia shot back.

Karina stuck out her tongue and stepped away. I happened to be near her when she whispered into her fingers and thought I heard her say, 'Karina the Stupendous', but I must have been mistaken. After all, she is such a modest, unassuming person.

Ryan's code phrase was 'Encyclopaedias are fun to read', which seemed to me a foolish phrase to choose for quagga-calling, since there was no chance one would ever say it accidentally. In fact, I wondered why anyone would even say it intentionally. Ryan punched my shoulder when I told him so, eliciting a spontaneous 'ow' from me, which kind of proved my point when Squig appeared without my having to consciously call her.

I was delighted to see my quagga again. After so many intervening events, it seemed like years since we parted, and on slightly strained terms too. I wondered if she was still angry with me for asking her to chew off my rope. Fortunately, she did not bear any grudge against me and soon we were speeding away together just like old times, though this time the ride was much bumpier. Thrice, I landed painfully on my buttocks. 'Badly paved cobblestones,' Squig explained cheerfully, though I noticed the other quaggas did not seem to have this difficulty.

It was a very good thing that, despite my having to waste time getting up from each fall, Squig was so fast, for the dragon was circling the skies above us, and no doubt would soon locate its prey if the quaggas had not spirited us away so quickly.

We dismissed our rides just before reaching the southern gate, where we paused while Karina prepped us for getting out of the city safely. 'The key to getting past the guards is to look confident and deny everything. They recognize me and will be sure to let you through if you keep quiet. You're lucky I'm with you!'

It seemed that the guards thought so too, for the moment we strode up to the gate, one of them shouted to his comrades, 'It's Karina! Good thing she's with the criminals, or it's highly likely we would not have recognized them. Arrest them all!'

'I deny everything!' I sang out, remembering Karina's earlier advice, but the guard only laughed and said, 'Save it for the interrogation. Arrest them all!'

'Wait! It must be a misunderstanding!' Karina cried.

'No misunderstanding,' the guard replied. 'We just received word that you're now an outlaw, like your father. Surrender peacefully or die!'

And then the guard appeared to shrivel up and fall down as if dead. And so did all his other fellows. Only then did I realize that they had all been attacked by a multitude of Krake-ropes.

I turned in surprise to see Mia standing in a very suave pose, an arm outstretched before her and another slightly to the back for balance. 'I love Krake-ropes! Best invention ever!' she chirped, clasping her hands together and stamping her feet in unbridled joy.

'You took all the tree branches from the cellar guard?' Karina asked. She looked like she was trying hard not to sound impressed and failing spectacularly.

'Yeah, didn't you notice?' she asked all of us.

'Er ... no,' we mumbled.

'Really?' she said incredulously. 'I had, like, eight branches sticking out of my belt.'

Karina and I were starting to murmur sheepish excuses when Ryan advised, 'Let's call our quaggas before the dragon gets here,' and we rushed to take his excellent advice.

'Karina the Stupendous!'

'Mia is awesome!'

'Encyclopaedias are fun to read!'

'Ow!'

***

We rode our respective whirlwinds back to the plains. This time, because we had exited the City of a Thousand Spires via its southern gate, we did not need to pass through the Golden Forest at all, which was a pity because I was starting to feel a little hungry. I fell five times ('uneven soil,' my kind steed took the trouble to explain to me), but eventually we all made it to the plains safely. Mia took out the sticker that had been magicked to remember the spot of the secret entrance and the last part of the journey was taken at a trot as the quaggas followed the sticker's wafting flight.

Eventually, the sticker drifted down and landed about ten metres away.

'Onward, girl!' I said heartily to Squig, my pulse quickening at the thought of soon being back in my own world.

'Yikes!' Squig replied, throwing me off her back and then galloping off faster than I could say: 'Why would you do such a thing? Why, why?'

The other three quaggas had run off as well, leaving my three friends standing and me sprawling on the grass in bewilderment.

'Well, it's not far to walk,' said Ryan.

While it was true that only ten metres of grass stood between us and our exit route, who knew what new dangers would be thrown our way?

As it happened, our quaggas had spotted the danger before we did, for we now saw the huge shadow moving over the plains towards us. Fearing the worst, we looked up into the sky to see what was making the shadow.

Dark clouds. It was going to rain.

'Didn't you say the weather here is always just nice?' Mia complained to Ryan.

'It usually is,' Karina said, sounding puzzled. Just then, a flash of lightning lit up the sky beyond the looming rain clouds. 'What's that?' she gasped, grabbing my arm.

'Lightning,' I explained. 'It's common when there's a storm.'

'But ... we never have storms here,' she said, sounding bewildered. 'Something must have caused it!'

'You mean ... something like that?' Ryan squeaked, and we all looked at where his trembling finger was pointing.

Accompanied by the rumble of distant thunder, a dragon was bursting through the clouds and streaking towards us like an arrow.

We all just stood there, stunned, for a second, then Mia yelled, 'Run!'

We made a beeline for the sticker on the ground. With my strength enhanced by magic, I could run twice as fast as my friends and had almost made it there when the dragon descended with a great deal of noisy wing-flapping and sat down, right on top of the sticker. I was so close to the dragon that I could smell its bad breath and armpit odour. Fortunately, it folded its wings, hiding its armpits, and thus left only the stench from its mouth for me to contend with. Very considerate beast.

We froze to a halt, me directly in front of the dragon and my friends a couple of metres behind. The dragon tossed its head indolently and looked at me with one eye. The good news was that it didn't seem in a hurry to eat me. The bad news was that it probably would, eventually.

'Retreat!' Karina hissed at me.

I put one foot behind me cautiously, but the dragon did not move. Maybe it was a friendly dragon and not in the employ of the CATTSS. But before I could turn tail and run, the air beside the dragon shimmered, and suddenly, there were eight old men and women standing beside it, and one old man sitting on the ground. They all wore grey or khaki-coloured robes and some were leaning on staffs for support. Accompanying them were a dozen guards attired in either city or citadel livery, each holding a tree branch.

'Teleportation makes me dizzy,' the old man on the ground wheezed.

'This had better be worth the Level Ten stickers,' one of the old women grumbled.

From their looks and numbers, I guessed that they must be the CATTSS councillors. The entire council, except for the ousted Wuchiwark, had come to witness my arrest. But it turned out that I was being too optimistic, for imprisonment was apparently too good for me.

One of the citadel guards stepped up to the youngest councillor, who looked about fifty and whose black hair stood out amid the ocean of white. 'The two kids with Karina are not the prophesied hero. I let them in through the back door myself when they were first caught. Their interrogators said the hero is their friend who escaped capture.'

The councillor stroked the dragon's flank as he levelled his piercing gaze at me. 'Then it must be you. Prepare to die.' Without taking his eyes off me, he said flatly, 'Draguni, my boy, kill him for me.'

'If you say so, Miaowi,' the dragon said lazily, his voice so deep and full of echoes that I almost couldn't make out the words. He yawned, showing off his crooked teeth. As he did so, understanding suddenly dawned on me. No wonder he had such bad breath! It must be difficult to brush such misaligned teeth.

I was still engrossed in examining the dental health of the creature when I realized that from the depth of Draguni's cavernous throat, somewhere just behind his quivering tonsils, a glowing orb was forming. The dragon was not yawning. He was readying his dragon fire!

'Run!' Mia screamed at me just as a blast of flame emerged from the dragon's mouth. There was no time to act or think. Even before it hit me, I could already feel the intense heat against my face like a sudden gust of desert wind.

Then, it did hit me, and just like that, it was all over.

Goodbye, sad world, I thought and then fell to the ground.

CHAPTER TWENTY-TWO

'Maybe he's not dead!' Mia said frantically, her voice choked with tears. 'Maybe he's just allergic to dragon fire!'

'There's no such allergy,' Karina said softly, sounding shell-shocked herself.

'We have failed. The quest is over,' Ryan moaned, for the second time that day.

For a dead person, I sure could hear the conversation around me clearly. I could even feel the cool earth under my body and the soft grass tickling my nose. Then realization struck me: I wasn't dead! I wasn't even hurt! (Except for the bruises accumulated from falling down the stairs into the swans' pantry, rolling down the steps at Yonder Bridge, and falling off Squig so many times.) I sprang to my feet in embarrassment and dusted myself off. 'I'm all right!' I called out. 'Just tripped over my feet trying to back away!'

I could not tell if my friends, the dragon or the councillors looked more shocked at my apparent resurrection.

'It can't be!' Draguni gasped. 'No one escapes my fire!' He took a deep breath and huffed out another fireball at me. This time, I was prepared and stood with my legs apart for balance, my arms akimbo. The fireball hit me in the chest, then plopped to the ground and fizzled out.

'What!' Draguni said, starting to look panicked. 'Have I lost my power?'

He started breathing out fireball after fireball, but I batted them away with my hands or let them fall off my body with no damage to myself at all. Soon, I was standing in a semi-circular patch of singed grass, but I had not a single burn on my body.

Cheers erupted from behind me as my friends realized I was impervious to the dragon's deadly attack.

'It's impossible!' the dragon wailed, then burst into tears. It was a piteous sight indeed, to see such a great creature brought so low. I almost offered to let him burn me just a little, so he would not lose all of his self-esteem, but I knew that if I peeled off the Level Nine sticker I had pasted on my chest during the Soothy Sisters' Spectacular Stunt Show, I would be burnt to a crisp in no time.

'Don't stop trying to kill him!' Miaowi rasped.

'But I can't!' Draguni bawled. Then, he extended his wings and took off, his tears falling over us like rain.

'Oh, it's rain,' the old woman who had spoken earlier now said, sounding surprised. The dark clouds had by now covered the entire sky and a light drizzle had started.

'Never upset a dragon,' another councillor said sagely as we all watched the majestic creature, now a wreck of his former self, slink off into the distant sky towards a reddish glow in the horizon.

'What's that?' Ryan asked, pointing.

'Probably his volcanic mountain home,' Karina guessed. 'I don't think the councillors will be making use of that dragon any time soon. His spirit is broken.'

'Good work on defeating the dragon, Ju,' Mia said admiringly. 'How did you do it?'

'Through my natural awesomeness, of course,' I said loudly, conscious that Miaowi was listening as well, which was why I chose to give such a plausible reason.

However, Miaowi did not look impressed. 'No matter!' he snarled. 'As a backup plan, I have prepared a spell specially to counter the hero from the Overworld. It is made from the magic of twenty Level Ten stickers and cannot be neutralized. Prepare to die ... again!'

Again? I groaned. I was going to need some serious therapy by the time this adventure was over. Unless they really managed to kill me. Was there therapy in the afterlife? I certainly hoped so. Maybe it would even be free! Wait a minute ... was there even an afterlife? Lost in my thoughts, I nearly missed seeing Miaowi pull a transparent flask out from inside his robes and give it a good shake. The clear liquid in the flask started to fizzle and bubble, and a yellow gas formed above the water level. He raised his other hand to pull the stopper out, but the old woman cried out, 'Stop! What if the gas poisons us all?'

'No fear,' Miaowi said, his lips twitching complacently. 'This spell is specially formulated to only harm one specific person. I've been brewing it for a decade, and now, we shall see what it can do.'

Mollified, the old woman stepped back, and Miaowi released the gas.

'Ow, ow, ow!' I cried hysterically, but Squig did not come. Neither did the other quaggas when my friends called them. They must have been too frightened of the dragon to return.

Mia, Ryan, Karina and I huddled together, fear gripping our hearts. We had no more stickers, no quaggas, no Krake-ropes, no pillows, and certainly no cookies. Nothing left with which to defend us or carry us away to safety. We could outrun the old folk but certainly not the dozen tall and strong guards on this open field. Or at least, I could, but my friends couldn't, and I had no intention of leaving them behind. In other words, we were doomed.

The yellow smoke rose up from the flask, its movements strangely uninhibited by the drizzle. It floated indeterminately for a few seconds, then started moving towards me.

Ryan gasped as a sudden thought occurred to him. 'Miaowi said the spell is made specially to counter the hero and no one else. Ju, quick run away! Don't worry about us. It won't harm us!'

He was right! I clamped my hands to my mouth and nose and took to my heels. It was hard to run and not breathe at the same time, so after a few seconds, I had to let in some air. Immediately, an overly sweet scent assailed my senses and I nearly gagged. The yellow smoke! It had followed me and now hung over my head like a cloud. Disoriented, I staggered about, holding my breath and trying not to vomit.

Then, out of the corner of my vision, I saw that Mia was doing a handstand and Ryan reading a book, as if they knew they had only a few seconds left to live and were determined to live their remaining lives to the utmost, doing the things they loved best. Once I understood that, the futility of it all struck me and I was filled with helpless rage. What was the point of delaying the inevitable? Better to have it over and done with! With that uplifting thought, I took away my hands and breathed in deeply.

The yellow haze shifted. I sniffed in its direction, but it resisted, pulling away instead. *What? Even the poison is bullying me, trying to drag out my ordeal so it could laugh at my pain?* I chased after it, trying to put my nose into its cloud, but it fled from me as if I were the poison and it the victim instead. If smoke had emotions, I could have sworn I saw it cast one last desperate glance back at me, then dissipate in a panic.

The smoke was gone. What had just happened? This time, I had to figure out if my friends and the councillors were more surprised, or I was, and just thinking about it was giving me a headache.

'But it's impossible!' Miaowi said, echoing the dragon's earlier reaction. 'The spell was targeted at Matthew Pane— the one and only Matthew Pane. It couldn't have failed! Wait a minute ...' Comprehension dawned on his face, and he turned to Ryan. 'What did you call him just now? "Ju", you said. Is that a short form for Matthew?' he asked hopefully.

'Er ... yes?' Ryan stammered, trying to keep up the bluff.

'He was saying "Hew", not "Ju",' Mia added helpfully.

'Oh well,' Miaowi said, recovering from his unexpected setback with admirable speed. 'It doesn't matter whether you're Matthew or not. What matters is that you're not leaving the Underworld with the Ef-frock.'

'Not answering to that name!' came Tago's sulky voice from Ryan's backpack.

Gasps erupted from the councillors. 'It can talk! How is it that it can talk?'

Miaowi tossed the now-empty flask behind him, and it promptly shattered on the ground. 'Enough quibbling about names!' he snarled. 'Ju, or Hew, or whoever you are, I'll just have to kill you the traditional way. Guards, get him, dead or alive! No, scratch that. Dead better than alive!'

The dozen guards saluted and readied their tree branches.

Just then, Ryan shouted, 'Wait! Don't you know the laws of dragon service?'

Miaowi gave a startled look. He had evidently forgotten the laws of dragon service and was only now recalling them. With an utterly guilty countenance, he said cloyingly, 'What laws? There are no laws. Guards—'

'Listen!' Ryan said, his usually weak voice now ringing with authority. 'Dragons may be bound to service by their tamers,' he read from the book in his hands, 'but if they ever meet a foe they are unable to vanquish, no one else may be allowed to harm that foe, for it is the dragons' prerogative to seek vengeance for that disgrace in their own time.'

As he spoke, Miaowi's face turned paler and paler. Some of the other councillors who had been oohing and aahing at the various turns of events now joined the old man on the ground and took out their picnic baskets so they could enjoy the unfolding drama in comfort.

'Where … where did you get that?' Miaowi stammered.

'This book?' Ryan said, showing us the cover which read, 'Ten Reasons Why Using Dragons to Kill Your Enemies is Not a Good Idea'. 'I found it in the citadel library. So, will you honour the contract you have with Draguni or not?'

'I will …' Miaowi paused, his eyes darting from side to side as he calculated his chances, then his expression cleared and he continued, ' … not! Draguni is not here. I'll tell him you choked on a cupcake and died. Guards—'

The tree branches were raised. *Oh no, here we go again,* I thought, starting to feel a little bored. How many times did we have to get threatened by Krake-ropes before the end of our adventure?

A puff of precisely-aimed fire incinerated all the tree branches in an instant, leaving the guards shaking their singed hands and cursing, and us with the assurance we would not be troubled by Krake-ropes for the rest of the adventure. Hopefully.

The overcast sky had camouflaged Draguni's approach, and now he landed lightly by my side. I made a valiant effort not to puke from his stench since he had just saved me. Fortunately, he folded his wings, thereby hiding his malodorous armpits.

Miaowi looked stunned and outraged, then quickly arranged his features into one of fawning benevolence. 'Come, Draguni,' he coaxed, bending down and patting the ground beside himself. 'Come over here to Papa.'

Draguni shook his massive head.

'Why did you return anyway?' Miaowi asked, his tone switching abruptly to annoyance as he straightened. 'I thought you'd gone off to sulk in your cave.'

'My home is spewing ashes. While the molten magma would make a very comfortable sauna, I cannot bear the haze. So, I come back here, and what do I see?' The dragon's deep voice was stern and admonishing. 'You are still trying to kill the hero who has managed to overcome the Great Draguni! How dare you! The hero is mine to kill. I must figure out a way to defeat him, or my shame will never be washed away. Until then, no one can harm him!'

'Yeah! High five!' I said jubilantly.

The dragon looked down at his humongous, clawed feet with razor-sharp nails as if wondering whether to humour me, and I quickly put down my hand. 'Never mind,' I mumbled.

'Fine,' Miaowi said. 'I won't kill him. I'll just imprison him, how about that?'

Draguni thought for a moment, then nodded. 'That seems fair—'

'No!' Ryan interjected.

The dragon twisted his neck to look at the boy who had dared to interrupt the Great Draguni.

Ryan appeared terrified at his own daring but continued bravely, 'Pardon me, O great dragon, but that wouldn't be right. If Julian is put into jail, he will become demoralized and depressed—'

'I knew it!' Miaowi cut in. 'He's not Matthew! No wonder the poison didn't work!'

Draguni gave Miaowi a withering look, and the councillor subsided into a chastised silence.

'Go on, boy,' the dragon intoned.

Ryan stuttered, 'Er … where was I? Oh, yes, demoralized and depressed. He will be unable to eat and become very weak. What honour is there in killing such a shell of a boy? No, he must be allowed to thrive. All the more glory to you when you finally vanquish him!'

'Hear, hear!' I chimed in grandly, because I had read of people saying that in books, although their audience usually ignored them, which was what happened now, to my disappointment.

'And his friends must go free as well,' Karina added quickly. 'If not, he will sadden and waste away.'

Draguni gave a low hoot. 'By the bones of my ancestors, you are right!' He turned back to Miaowi. 'You hear that? No imprisonment! The boy and his friends must be free to go where they will!'

'But he means to go to the Overworld!' Miaowi's voice had risen half an octave in his agitation.

The dragon waved a claw dismissively. 'No matter where he goes, I will find him, when the time is right.'

Miaowi was so tensed up that all the veins on his face and neck throbbed prominently. 'All right,' he said through clenched teeth in a supreme display of self-control. 'But he must leave behind the Ef-frock that he has stolen.'

'Not answering to that name,' said Tago in a tired voice.

'No!' Ryan said. 'We need the Ef-frock as collateral.'

'Not answering to that name,' repeated Tago, though his heart did not seem to be in it any more. He seemed to be objecting simply as a matter of principle.

'Otherwise,' Ryan continued, 'what assurance do we have that we won't be harmed once we leave the Great Draguni's august presence?'

'You hear that?' Draguni boomed to Miaowi.

The dragon seemed in the mood to support our every proposal, so I tossed in my own condition as well: 'And we must be given the jar of cookies in the guardian swans' pantry, else we might starve to death before getting home.'

'Sounds reasonable,' Draguni said approvingly.

Perspiration was beginning to bead on Miaowi's forehead. While he had behaved high and mighty all this time, he now sounded desperate as he pleaded, 'Please, Julian, you don't understand. I know why you want to take the Ef-frock—'

'Not answering to that name.'

'—to the Overworld, but you don't know what harm to our world you'll be causing.'

In the face of Miaowi's distress, I hesitated, but Mia snapped, 'Don't be conned by him, Ju. He's just trying to confuse you.'

She was right. I shook off my uneasiness and said, 'Don't worry, once my world is saved, we'll return the Ef-frock to your world.'

We all paused to wait for Tago to interject, but he appeared to have fallen asleep.

'No,' Miaowi moaned. 'It'll be too late by then.'

The other councillors had been content to let Miaowi handle the situation so far, but now they began to murmur restively among themselves.

'What can Miaowi mean?'

'Is there really some danger we don't know about?'

'Or is he just trying to pull a fast one on the kids?'

'Can you pass the potato chips?'

Miaowi munched on a chip glumly. He seemed deflated, all the intensity gone out of his carriage. Instead, all I saw was an old man heavy with too many cares. He covered his face with one hand and waved us on with the other. 'Go,' he said. 'Perhaps it is fated to be so.'

I nodded, wishing there was some way I could comfort him that did not involve my death or imprisonment. After thinking for a bit, I said, 'I hope you are enjoying your potato chips.'

At that, he burst into wild sobbing. He must have been very touched by my words. I hadn't realized I had said something that profound.

'Farewell, noble hero,' Draguni said solemnly to me.

'Thank you,' I replied. 'You are an honourable dragon. I will never forget you.'

'One day, we will meet again. I will not rest until I discover the way to defeat you, even if it takes me a hundred years.'

'A hundred years sounds about right to me,' I assured him.

Draguni escorted us to the sticker that was still magically marking the location of the secret door. It took us a while, but we managed to find the tell-tale circular groove in the soil and lift the hatch. The guardian swans' small lounge room got quite crowded with four kids and nine councillors, not to mention the dragon's eye peering down at us from the hole above, but no one wanted to miss the rare and momentous occasion of three Overworlders and an Underworlder sliding down the chute connecting our two worlds.

Even in the crush, I did not forget to put the hard-won jar of cookies in my bag. Then, the four of us stood before the slide, the Ef-frock still safely stowed in Ryan's backpack. I almost could not believe that we had got this far in our quest, but managed to do so with some effort.

'I can't believe we got so far in our quest!' Ryan said, sounding a little dazed.

'Try putting in some effort,' I said encouragingly.

Mia had a broad grin on her face. 'We sure aced the mission, didn't we?' Then she glanced at her watch. 'Warring warriors!' she exclaimed. 'It's almost 8 p.m.!'

I hadn't realized it was so late, what with the eternal sunlight in the Underworld. 'We were supposed to meet Wuchiwark at 7 p.m.!' I said in dismay.

And even though this was such a pivotal moment in our adventure, and deserved a longer duration where we shared with each other the flurry of emotions and thoughts running through our heads, I knew there was no time.

'We have to go now! Bye!' I said with a backward wave to the councillors, then hopped on to the slide. We were finally on our way home.

CHAPTER TWENTY-THREE

The return trip was similar to the first, except that while I had come to a gentle rest on a very comfortable mattress in the Underworld, now I fell into a prickly bush. I'm pretty sure this was symbolic of a certain difference between our worlds, but I'm not sure exactly what. Maybe our ability to grow more prickly plants.

A flash of lightning lit up the night sky, and I found myself staring into the eyes of Horace, the guardian swan. Or it could be Ovid. No, it was Horace. The swan's neck was pure white. I waited for it to speak, but it just squawked and waddled away. It was an ordinary swan.

'Where are the guardian swans?' Ryan asked. He had just shot out of the slide.

'I don't know,' I replied. Another streak of lightning flashed across the sky, followed by the rumble of distant thunder, reminding us that the end of the world was nigh.

We were soon joined by Mia. 'Where are the guardian swans?' she asked.

This time, I wizened up. 'Wait,' I told her.

Finally, Karina arrived. 'So this is your world,' she marvelled, looking around her. 'But where are the guardian swans?'

'I don't know,' I said efficiently to both Mia and Karina at the same time.

'Is it always this humid?' Karina asked, dabbing at her forehead with her sleeve as we walked along the path beside Swan Lake. We were headed towards Tanglin Gate in the east, where we would be able to catch a bus to the music centre.

'No,' Mia assured her. 'Quite often, it's worse. You probably won't survive long here.'

It was nice to see the two of them getting along.

'We were supposed to meet Wuchiwark at the music centre more than an hour ago,' Ryan said. 'Do you think he'll still be there?'

Before I could reply, we heard sounds of scuffling coming from behind some fronds beside the path.

'Stop kicking!' came Horace's voice.

'What I wouldn't give for a Krake-rope,' Ovid sighed.

I gave a start. The swans were just a couple of metres away from us!

'You know we're not supposed to use magic in the Overworld, so quit complaining,' Horace's voice rang out. 'Quick, finish with the weaving.'

More scuffling noises.

The four of us tiptoed past the bush, grateful the swans were occupied with something else—art and craft, from the sounds of it—and we could slip away quietly.

'Done!' came Ovid's relieved voice. 'I hope it's long enough.'

'You know those reeds aren't going to hold me,' said a third voice, which stopped us in our tracks. It was Wuchiwark!

'Oh, it'll hold you long enough for one of us to escort you to the Underworld,' Horace assured him.

So Wuchiwark had been captured! That sure put a spanner in our plans. Who else would know how to activate the Ef-frock to save our world?

'We have to rescue him!' Mia whispered.

'But how?' I whispered back. 'We don't want to fight the invincible guardian swans!'

'Who wants to fight us?' Horace asked, stepping out from behind the fronds that had been hiding him from view. Ovid followed, pulling on a leash in his beak. Wuchiwark was dragged along, and he soon came into view. His hands were tied and attached to Ovid's leash, and he looked grumpy and dishevelled. Otherwise, he did not seem to have been harmed.

'Er … actually, what I said was that we *don't* want to fight you,' I corrected the swan.

'Julian!' Wuchiwark brightened up when he saw me, then his brow creased into a frown. 'Karina, what are you doing here?'

'Your gang recruited me,' she replied.

'What gang?' he asked, a blank look on his face. 'I don't know any gang.'

'*His* gang!' Karina said, pointing at me and glaring at her father.

'Who is he?' Wuchiwark said without missing a beat. 'I don't know him. Oh, and I don't know you either, by the way.'

'What's going on?' Mia asked impatiently.

Ryan gripped my arm. 'I think he's lost his marbles,' he said worriedly.

'Didn't have any to begin with!' Wuchiwark said cheerfully.

The swans had been listening to our exchange with interest, and now Horace said, 'Come, Wuchiwark, denying possession of marbles will not get you out of this.'

Wuchiwark put on a puzzled expression. 'I've been telling and telling you that I'm not this Wuchi-whatever guy you've been going on about. You've got the wrong person.'

Horace shook a wing at him. 'I'll recognize you anywhere, Wuchiwark. You presented Ovid and me with our 'Steadfastness in a Boring Job' award at last year's Excuses for Celebration Festival.'

Wuchiwark chuckled, his eyes dreamy with reminiscence. 'That was a fun event,' he sighed, then recollected himself. 'I mean, that sounds like it could have been a fun event, especially if there were roasted marshmallows.'

'There *were* roasted marshmallows!' Ovid exclaimed triumphantly.

'That only proves we like the same snack,' Wuchiwark remarked. 'It doesn't prove I'm who you think I am.'

Horace pointed to me with an outstretched wing, and I tried to school my expression into one of cherubic innocence. 'Don't you think we know by now that this boy sneaked into the Underworld under your instigation?' the swan said in an accusatory tone. 'Don't pretend you don't know him. You called him by name!'

'Merely a lucky guess,' Wuchiwark said with a casual wave of his bound hands. 'There are only so many names a boy could have.'

'So you claim to know nothing about the Underworld?' Horace demanded.

'What Underworld?' Wuchiwark lied smoothly. 'I only know of one world, which is where we are now!'

'If you belong to this world as you claim,' Horace said, a glint in his eye, 'then you will have no problem answering our three test questions.'

'Test questions?' Wuchiwark blinked, looking confused.

Horace nodded. 'If you are able to answer three questions about this world correctly, we will believe that you are not who we believe you are.'

Wuchiwark gulped. 'Fire away,' he said bravely, though his quivering beard betrayed his anxiety.

There was no doubt that he would get the questions all wrong. I was certain that Wuchiwark was only going through with this charade to buy us some time to think of a way out. But how? I looked at my friends, but they were as helpless as I was.

Horace began, 'First question. Complete this idiom: "The world is your …"'

Wuchiwark's cheeks flushed in suppressed delight. 'Oyster, of course,' he said with an extravagantly nonchalant air. 'Why? Did you think it was a fruit?'

My friends and I cheered and exchanged high fives.

Horace scowled, which on a swan looked like he was trying to break his upper beak on his lower. 'Second question,' he pushed on resolutely. 'What is Dr Seuss? This is a really hard one so I will give you some options. A: a doctor. B: a writer. C: a prawn.'

Wuchiwark's grin was so wide it could have split his face into two. 'A writer. Have you tried his green eggs and ham?'

The swans looked astounded. Ovid's jaw dropped (meaning, he opened his beak), and the reed-leash fell to the ground.

'Only one last question!' Mia crowed.

'Might as well start untying him to save time!' I chimed in, moving towards Wuchiwark. I was certain he would get the last question wrong. There was only so much he could have learnt about the Overworld in the two days he was here. If I could free him from his binds, perhaps we could try to outrun the swans since they had such puny legs. Wait a minute … could swans fly?

'Not so fast!' Horace stepped between me and the old man, blocking my move. 'Third question. Who is the president of the Overworld?' he demanded.

It was a trick question! There was no such person! Unlike the Underworld, which was one big happy family, our world was divided into countries and each nation had its own leader. I tried to convey all that to Wuchiwark through eye blinks and mouth twitches, but sadly, mind-reading did not appear to be his forte.

Wuchiwark pulled at his beard miserably. He knew he was beaten, and it showed on his face. 'Er … you?' he said, a valiant effort at humour when all was so clearly lost.

The swans stared at each other in astonishment. They had probably never heard such a ludicrous answer in their lives. Then, very slowly, they began to clap: their feathered wings made no sound, but we all got the general idea.

'Ingenious!' Ovid marvelled.

'He understands this world so well!' Horace agreed. 'Our answer was "nobody", but he gave an even better response than ours. He knows that no human being in the Overworld is good enough to be president, and that if things were as they should be, the president should be a swan!'

Ovid began loosening the reed-leash with his beak, while Horace apologized, 'We're terribly sorry, old chap. We mistook you for a villainous turncoat from our world, not knowing you are a great man of this land.'

'I forgive you,' Wuchiwark said generously. 'It's a boring job you have and you deserve every bit of excitement you can get. I'm surprised you don't catch more people wrongly just for the fun of it.'

Horace sighed. 'You don't know the half of it. We've been having a bad run recently. We would capture Julian and his gang now, if not for his army of six hundred soldiers.'

'I don't have—' I said, but Ryan shushed me by kicking me in the shin, which I thought was very rude of him.

'Yeah,' Ovid chipped in. 'Since we were unable to defeat their army when we first encountered them, it would be really odd if we managed to capture those kids now. One might even question if there was such an army in the first place.'

'Which there is,' Horace said firmly.

'Oh yes, there definitely is,' Mia confirmed. 'How else could we have got into the Underworld? Certainly not by tricking such mighty guardians as yourselves.'

'Hear, hear,' Ovid said, nodding. He must have read the same books as me.

The swans bade us a fond farewell, and I made a mental note never to come to Swan Lake again without a disguise.

***

Karina had appeared delighted when her father had passed the swans' test, but now, as we walked away from the lake together, I noticed she tried to keep as far away from him as possible, and answered his questions with just grunts or monosyllables.

Finally giving up on trying to engage his daughter, Wuchiwark turned to us. 'So, I take it you managed to get the Ef-frock?'

Ryan patted his backpack. 'Right here,' he said, whereupon we gave him an account of our adventures in the Underworld, minus all the embarrassing bits. I was surprised it took us only half a minute, considering all that we had been through.

'Good!' he replied. 'You came back just in time. Any later and boom! Your world would have been gone. The lightning has been going on for the whole day, and I heard the volcanoes are close to erupting. Now, just bring me to a picturesque place and I will activate the rock.'

'Does it have to be picturesque?' asked Mia, who did not care for pretty things.

'Don't you know magic always works better when the environment looks nice?' Wuchiwark said as he stroked his white eyebrows. 'The peak of a snow-capped mountain, a lone pavilion in the middle of a huge lake, a ragged sea-facing cliff where you could time the activation with a massive wave … any of these will do. I'm not fussy.'

'We don't have any of that in Singapore,' Ryan said apologetically. 'We're quite a flat island and rather small too. There are a number of gazebos in the Botanic Gardens, but they're just ordinary rest areas and nothing like what you described.'

Clearly disappointed he would not have a beautiful backdrop for his display of magic, Wuchiwark pulled himself together with visible effort. 'Well, an ugly gazebo is better than nothing. Lead the way!'

Ryan obediently moved to the front of the group. As we walked, Mia asked, 'How did you get caught by the swans?'

Wuchiwark sounded aggrieved as he recounted, 'I was waiting for you at the music centre, but you were late.'

'It wasn't like we did it on purpose,' Mia said defensively.

'That's what you say,' Wuchiwark grumbled. 'I hung around for twenty-nine minutes, then decided to come here to look for you. So stealthy was I that even the formidable guardian swans did not hear my approach. I settled down in some bushes near the secret entrance to wait. And then, a yawn crept up on me.'

Noticing the amused smiles on our lips, Wuchiwark puffed up indignantly. 'I haven't slept in two days, since I can't stay in one place for longer than half an hour. So, I yawned. As I'm sure you know, quiet yawns make you more tired while loud yawns invigorate you. I really had no choice in the matter. Suffice it to say that I was not the only one invigorated by my yawn. Ah, is that the gazebo?'

It was quite a pretty one, actually: an octagonal pavilion with white, latticed supports and a steeply sloping brown tiled roof. It was surrounded by a ring of Yellow Rain Trees, giving the whole scene a rather ethereal feel. A couple of wooden benches on the stone floor inside the gazebo, arranged so that the centre was left empty, were its only ornament. Wuchiwark rubbed his palms in delight. The gazebo had clearly exceeded his expectations aesthetically.

Ryan upended his backpack in the centre and the Ef-frock popped out, immediately reverting to its original size, all red and green and shimmery, like it had been in the maze.

We stepped back and watched as Wuchiwark stood before the Ef-frock, readying himself for the powerful magic. Then, he placed his hands on the rock and intoned in a sing-song voice, getting louder with each syllable until the last couple of words were practically shouted: 'Abracadabra, hokey pokey, hey presto, hocus-pocus, open sesame!'

We waited with bated breath for the moment of power to descend upon the world.

The dark sky flickered with the glow of distant lightning. The Ef-frock gleamed quietly.

But there was no moment of power.

Nothing had changed.

It was as if we had never brought back the rock at all.

CHAPTER TWENTY-FOUR

Wuchiwark staggered a little with the shock, then found the bench behind him and sat down in a daze. 'Impossible!' he muttered, staring at his hands. 'The spell should have worked. What went wrong?'

'Maybe you said the wrong words?' I suggested.

'In the wrong order?' Mia said.

'With the wrong inflexion?' Ryan proposed.

'Shh!' Wuchiwark hushed us irritably.

I figured the old man needed some time to think through what to do next, so I quit bothering him and took out my jar of cookies for a snack to while away the time.

'Good thinking to ask for the cookies, Ju,' Ryan said.

'Yeah, good job. I'd forgotten about it myself,' Mia added in a rare instance of self-deprecation.

I hadn't realized my friends were also so keen on the cookies. I hoped this didn't mean I would have to share them.

Karina nodded. 'It might have been impossible to get Tago to come out otherwise.'

Oh, Tago! 'Yeah, that's what I thought too,' I mumbled.

'Did someone say cookies?' There was a slight blurring in the air and Tago materialized, taking the place of the rock. He grabbed the cookie in my hand and began munching without ceremony.

'Hello, Tago,' Wuchiwark said glumly.

'Hi, old chap,' Tago replied with a familiarity that surprised me for a moment before I remembered that Wuchiwark was one of the only two people in the Underworld who had known Tago's true identity from the start.

'Looks like you can't save this world after all,' Wuchiwark commented.

'Yeah,' said Tago nonchalantly as he helped himself to another cookie. 'Especially since I don't have any magic any more.'

'What?' all of us chorused, simultaneously stabbing him with our dagger eyes.

'But … but … you're the Ef-frock!' Karina protested. 'The Ever Rock! How can you have no magic?'

'Papa said to keep it a secret, but I suppose there's no harm telling you now,' Tago said as he munched.

Wuchiwark narrowed his eyes. 'Miaowi knows about it?'

'Of course,' Tago said. 'Why do you think he banned the use of stickers in the citadel and limited the number issued to the population?'

'Because he is an evil overlord?' Karina said dryly.

'You're just prejudiced,' Tago retorted. 'Thirteen years ago, when I first took human form, the powers of my rock form disappeared. Papa deduced that my first metamorphosis required so much magic that there was none left after that. The only magic I can perform now is to change between my two forms.'

'And Miaowi never told me?' Wuchiwark sounded both incredulous and indignant.

'It's the sort of thing that the fewer people know the better. Since Papa was solely in charge of extracting my magic into stickers, he decided that no one else needs to know. It would cause unnecessary panic among the people.'

Wuchiwark nodded slowly. 'I can understand that. There would be widespread panic if they found out magic might soon be a thing of the past. Worse still, they may no longer trust the CATTSS to run the world. Society will break down into factions once they are no longer willing to submit to the laws of the council. The factions might war with each other and form separate nations ...'

The old man gave a gasp and stared at us Overworlders in horror as the true enormity of the situation struck him. 'We might end up becoming like you!'

We looked at each other and squirmed uncomfortably. 'Oh, we're not so bad,' Ryan said lamely.

'I'll pretend I didn't hear that,' Wuchiwark said, patting Ryan's shoulder comfortingly. Turning back to Tago, he said, 'I did think it odd when he suddenly implemented his sticker reforms. I remember he announced that a reduction in sticker distribution was necessary for the people's good. It was such an obvious con that he wouldn't have got away with it if he hadn't muddled the issue with babble like "developing life skills" and "mindset change".'

'But developing life skills and having the ability to change your mindset are important,' Ryan insisted. 'My parents say their bosses tell them that all the time!'

Wuchiwark grinned. 'Point proven,' he said, leaving poor Ryan dumbfounded.

Mia, meanwhile, had been keeping her mind on the issue at hand. 'Even with a reduction in sticker distribution, Miaowi still needs to get the stickers from somewhere.'

Tago nodded. 'These past thirteen years, he has been drawing on the citadel's stockpile of stickers for distribution, while keeping my inability to produce new stickers a secret.'

Wuchiwark commented, 'That's easy enough for him to do since he takes care of the citadel's reserves.'

'Seems like Miaowi's been doing all the work for the council,' Mia said. 'Do you and the other councillors do any work at all?'

Wuchiwark cleared his throat. 'Lots,' he affirmed, though his eyes looked a bit shifty when he said that. 'So!' he said to Tago in a jolly voice before we could question him further. 'Do continue with your very interesting tale!'

'There's not much more. With my magic gone, there's no way I can save the Overworld. Once this world is destroyed despite my presence here, everyone will know about my loss of powers and chaos will befall our world. That's why Papa tried to stop you from bringing me here.'

Phrases that Miaowi had said came to my mind and took on a new meaning. *You don't know what harm to our world you'll be causing … It'll be too late …*

'That's the real reason he tried to stop us?' I asked, suddenly feeling sorry for the poor man who had carried such a heavy burden by himself for so long.

'What, did you think it was because he wanted your world to die so he could have a clean slate to send prisoners to?' Tago snapped.

'Um … that thought never did cross my mind,' I stammered.

Karina, who had been listening quietly all this while, gave a start as something occurred to her. 'Did the Soothy brothers' murders have to do with this secret?'

Tago shifted uneasily. 'They weren't killed outright. They just didn't quite take to the smell of socks. But yeah, they came early to set up for a citadel performance and overheard me and

Papa talking. They couldn't be allowed to go out and spread the news.'

At the look of outrage on Karina's face, Tago said stubbornly, 'It was all for the greater good. Sssss sounds much nicer than Ss-brr-sss. Anyway, Papa just needs some time to find a way to restore my power. Once I regain my power, everything will be all right again.'

Karina looked like she was about to explode. She pointed at Tago with a trembling finger and challenged her father, 'And you expect me to marry such a scumbag?'

Wuchiwark shook his head. 'There's no need now. I only agreed to the betrothal in the first place so that I can have close access to the Ef-frock. I thought that when the time of the prophecy came, I would be able to take the rock to save the Overworld. I never intended you to marry Tago at all.'

'Really?' Karina and Tago said in unison, though Karina's tone was filled with jubilation and Tago's with dismay.

Wuchiwark nodded. 'I didn't expect to be branded an outlaw the moment I resigned my position as councillor. I knew I had to flee the Underworld in a hurry before word got to the guardian swans about my status and I was no longer allowed to leave. There wasn't time to steal the Ef-frock or even to explain matters to you.'

Tago looked so miserable that I felt compelled to comfort him. 'Cookie?' I said in commiseration, and his eyes lit up with gratitude. He looked much better after that dose of sugar. I wondered whether stones could get diabetes.

'So our world is doomed,' Ryan said glumly.

'Cookie?' I offered him as well, but he only shook his head sadly.

To be honest, I wasn't feeling very perky myself. Could it really be that we had gone through all those dangers for nothing?

But what of the prophecy that foresaw a hero saving the world with the Ef-frock? Then again, the prophecy had named Matthew Pane. It was not me. It had never been meant to be me. Our quest had been doomed the moment Matthew fell with that first lightning strike.

The wind was rising, sending a ghostly howl that whistled through the gardens. The end could not be far now.

The rain started suddenly, without warning. One moment, there was only lightning and the next, great sheets of water were pounding the ground. Luckily, we were sheltered in the gazebo, though the lashing wind ensured that some wetness still managed to get in. The rain was so heavy that we could not see more than a few metres into it, which was a very good justification for why I yelped and jumped behind Mia when a white, feathery form suddenly blustered out of the storm and hurled itself into our pavilion.

'Horace!' Ryan said, recognizing the swan. 'What are you doing here?'

Fortunately, swans have waterproof feathers, so other than sopping the floor with great puddles of water, Horace did not appear to be much harmed by the storm. Yet, his entire demeanour had changed. While he had previously been pompous and proud, now his eyes were glazed with panic as he panted, 'I was sent to look for Julian!'

'Sent?' I asked, peeking out from behind Mia.

'Yes, an urgent message from Miaowi. Julian, you have to help us! Our world is dying!'

'You mean *our* world is dying,' I corrected him.

'No, I mean *our* world is dying,' Horace insisted. He recited:

When the mountains weep blood,
And the sky explodes with light,
When the winds bring seas to land—

'Turns out that the prophecy was referring to our world too! Inactive volcanoes are now spewing ash, lightning is striking everywhere, and our seas are rising!'

'No!' Karina exclaimed.

'Yes!' Ryan said, equally excited. 'It makes sense! That's why it was raining when we left, and Draguni said his mountain was acting up too!'

'I knew it!' Wuchiwark exclaimed, even though he clearly had not known it. 'I did wonder why a prophecy that originated from the Underworld should concern itself with another world, except that there are never any natural disasters down below, so everyone assumed it had to be referring to the Overworld.'

'I'm sorry for all of you,' I said, thinking in particular of the new friends I had made that day and left behind—Big and Small Soothy, Squig, and even Draguni. 'But there's nothing I can do. I'm not the original hero of the prophecy. Besides, the Ef-frock has lost all its magic. Miaowi knows that.'

'Yes, yes,' Horace said, desperation making his feathers hang heavy, or maybe it was just the weight of all that rainwater dripping off him. 'Miaowi explained everything in his message. But he said that since you were heroic enough to survive all the trials in the Underworld, surely you will be able to find a way. Miaowi added that you should look for Wuchiwark and perhaps the two of you together can find a solution.'

'But Wuchiwark is a wanted criminal,' Ryan said cautiously.

'Miaowi promised to grant Wuchiwark immunity if he agreed to help.'

Wuchiwark cleared his throat and stood up. 'How lucky it is then that I happened to run into these kids while taking a leisurely stroll in the Botanic Gardens! By the way, I heard you caught the wrong guy just now. Quite the embarrassment for you, eh?'

Horace stared at Wuchiwark and scratched his feathery head with a wing. 'Yeah, it was really awkward. You can't blame us though. You two looked really alike. He was even wearing the same clothes. Right, now that I've passed on the message, I have to get back to Ovid. He's a bit nervous guarding the entrance all by himself, what with the state of the worlds now.'

We watched as Horace plunged back into the storm and was soon obscured by the rain.

'What should we do?' Karina asked the moment the swan was gone.

'I suppose we should all go home and write our wills,' Ryan said gloomily, 'even though there won't be anyone left to leave our stuff to.'

'Or any stuff to leave,' Mia added.

For a minute, we stood brooding quietly over our imminent demise, the silence in the gazebo broken only by the incessant beats of the terrible downpour and the crunching of cookies. Tago was still working his way steadily through my jar.

Suddenly, he made a strangled sound and clutched his throat. His face turned beetroot red, and his eyes looked as if they were about to pop out of their sockets.

'He's choking!' Ryan exclaimed. He rushed over and slapped Tago on his back several times, to no avail.

'Let me try!' Karina said. She banged her fist hard enough to shatter a brick, but Tago still clawed at his throat desperately, tears streaming out of his eyes.

'Quick, someone try the Heimlich manoeuvre!' Ryan recommended.

I had no idea how hind-licking could help, but Mia responded with alacrity. 'Okay! What do I do?'

'Get behind him and push hard under his chest,' Ryan instructed.

Mia wrapped her arms around Tago and positioned her fist carefully on his abdomen. She was about to perform the first thrust when all of the sudden, she was no longer hugging a person, but a rock.

CHAPTER TWENTY-FIVE

The Ef-frock glowed alternately green and red as it sat there in the middle of the gazebo. Mia knocked on it with her fist. 'Hello?' she called.

No answer.

'Are you still alive?' she asked.

Nothing.

And then I guess Wuchiwark got his beautiful backdrop after all, for the storm outside started to swirl round the pavilion, creating in our sanctuary an epicentre of calm within the storm. We felt our hair whip against our faces. Fallen leaves were caught by the eddy and spun with the wind in a blur of white and brown. The column of wind rose up as high as we could see, and then, all of the sudden, it came rushing in at us from all sides. We dove to the ground to avoid the onslaught, though perhaps there was no need for such inelegant behaviour (Wuchiwark had scuttled under a bench with surprising agility for such an old man), for the storm appeared to be targeting the Ef-frock specifically and left the rest of us alone.

In fact, the winds and rain were not so much attacking the rock, as attracted by it. They hit the Ef-frock at incredible speeds and were immediately sucked into a multicoloured vortex that was spinning rapidly just under the now-translucent surface of the rock.

The phenomenon, while pretty, went on for far too long, in my opinion. Sometime in the middle of the display, I nodded off, and when I woke up and wiped the drool from the corner of my lips, the wind was just settling down and the night air smelt fresh and crisp.

The Ef-frock shimmered for several more seconds, then the whirlpool within it dissipated. The rock dissolved and there was Tago, sitting on the floor with a startled look on his face.

'What was that all about?' Karina asked.

Tago raised his hands and looked at them in wonderment, then gazed down all over his body. 'I think I just absorbed the power of a thousand storms and a hundred volcanoes!' he said in awe.

'How did you do that?' Wuchiwark asked, crawling out from under the bench.

'I don't know. All I remember was choking on a cookie and panicking, then suddenly I was taking in all this power!'

Wuchiwark snapped his fingers. 'It's the law of self-preservation!' he said excitedly. 'You didn't know how to consciously take power from the elements, but when you were in danger, your body automatically reached out for magic in order to save you. And you ended up absorbing all the energy that has been overwhelming the world!' He turned to the rest of us and announced, 'Congratulations! You have completed your quest! Your world is saved!'

'The end,' I added gratefully.

'No, wait …' Karina said. 'What about *our* world?'

'Oh, that's not a problem,' Tago said. 'Now that I've regained my powers, I can easily stop all that nonsense.'

'Oh, cool!' Karina said, which was probably the nicest thing she had ever said to Tago, for he turned a deep crimson and looked like he might go hide behind his rock facade again if I had not offered him a cookie.

Karina turned to Mia, Ryan and me. 'Once we've cleaned up the mess down below, do come and visit! I'll be your tour guide for real this time.'

Mia and Ryan nodded eagerly, and I thought with equal enthusiasm about the roast beef trees and juicy turkey legs. 'I would love that!' I said.

Karina looked thrilled. 'It's a date!'

Wuchiwark took my hand and shook it heartily. 'Thank you, Julian. If you hadn't given Tago the cookie to choke on, he might never have regained his powers. You have truly saved both our worlds by your heroic action!'

Ryan poked me in the back at the same time that Mia pinched my arm and Karina stomped on my toe. When I turned to face them, all three gave me meaningful looks, pointed at themselves, and jerked their chins at Wuchiwark. What was it they wanted me to tell him? Oh, they were probably urging me to be as humble as themselves in not taking credit for the successful mission. I turned back to Wuchiwark to explain.

'It's not all because of me,' I began, and my friends gave me encouraging nods. 'It's also Matthew Pane. He's the original hero of the prophecy. If not for him, you would not have met me. So, he really did save the world—by leading you to me!'

'You are right!' Wuchiwark marvelled. 'So the prophecy did come true after all! Well done, Julian!'

I grinned and turned back to give my friends the thumbs-up sign. Done! Just as they had suggested for me to do! I don't know why they all looked so sour.

'We should get going,' Wuchiwark said to Tago and Karina. 'We still have another world to save.'

'Will you be getting Miaowi to release Wuchichoc?' Ryan asked.

'I'll try,' Wuchiwark promised, 'but it may not be so straightforward. Although we now know Miaowi had good reasons for what he did, his measures still show how draconian he is by nature. It may take some time before the rest of us manage to wrest back some of the power we gave him. But don't worry. At the very least, I'll make sure they give Choc back his hot tub. Come on, Karina, Tago.'

'Can I ride in someone's backpack?' Tago wheedled.

'Sure!' Karina said cheerfully and popped open hers, whereupon Tago jumped up, transformed into the Ef-frock, and disappeared deep within the folds of the bag. Now that Karina no longer had to marry Tago, she seemed not to mind him so much. I guess it was like not minding a stomach ache when it wasn't yours.

'You do realize,' Mia said dryly to Wuchiwark, 'that if you'd thought to tell us that Tago is the Ef-frock, we could have completed the mission at Botuni's shop early in the day, without having to endanger our lives at all.'

The old man's eyes sparkled with merriment. 'Ah, but then you would have missed out on all the character building, friendship bonding, and stuff like that. No, no, no. If you are to go on a quest, you need to do it properly. Otherwise, there's no point doing it at all.'

'I thought the point was to save our world?' Ryan remarked.

'That too,' the old man said with a chuckle as he took Karina's hand and walked away from us. 'That too!'

THE END

Acknowledgements

Writing a book and seeing it through from manuscript to publication is tough. I think I'd rather pet a very cute bunny. I don't know why I keep doing it. Writing, I mean. Not petting bunnies. I think it must be the fault of the following people, because, without them, pursuing this path would have been impossible.

My mother, who gave me the best gift of all as a child—the love for reading.

My father, whose tiny collection of classic books became my staple when we were between visits to the library, and I simply had to read even if it was a book I'd read a million times.

My brother, who introduced me to the joy (and pain) of gamebooks, in particular, *Lone Wolf* and *GrailQuest*, which were great influences when I wrote *Prophecy of the Underworld*.

My husband, whose antics inspired the pillows-and-cats sequences in the book.

My daughter, who inspired everything else.

My bestie, Yipei, for being with me every step of this incredible journey.

The kid lit writing community in Singapore—surely the nicest and warmest bunch of people you can find—for their friendship and support, especially Hwee Goh, who keeps me sane with her endless optimism and an equally endless supply of books.

Associate Publisher Nora Nazerene, for being the first to believe in this book; and editor Amberdawn Manaois, for her insightful suggestions.

And all the other wonderful folk at the PRH SEA family who helped make this book a reality.

I can't thank you all enough. Cookie?